Rose from the
Bayou

Teryn Williams

First printing August 2012

ISBN-13: 978-0615690704
PUBLISHED BY TERYN WILLIAMS.
Printed in the U.S.A.

"Those who *matter don't mind,* and *those* who mind don't *matter."* –Dr. Seuss

To my favorite cop.
Always there to protect and serve.

Scarlet Rose Laveau

I was born right after midnight on October 31, 1970, beneath an orange moon. It was harvest time in New Orleans and I came into the world ready to feed all of those that dared to cross my path. My loving and doting parents named me Scarlet Rose, because a rose by any other name would have been less suitable.

A rose was the very first thing I ever had the pleasure in watching die. I took it from Nana's garden. It was the prettiest rose of all roses and I cut it from the vine all by myself. I knew without water it would suffer a quick death and so I took it home and laid it on my pillow. I did not want to miss a thing. The petals went limp first and then turned dark and eventually the rose dried all up and fell apart. I held the pieces of the rose in my hand and then crumpled it forgetting all about the thorns. The sharpness of the thorns was quick but painful and caused blood to drip from my small hands. I never cried over such things, pain was a part of life and you got out of it what you put into it. I smiled at the once rose now bloody in defeat. "The rose is dead, the rose is dead, the rose is dead." I repeatedly chanted while twirling in a circle.

Daddy Laveau gave me a kitten for my ninth birthday. I had already gone through several pets by then. There had been a bird, a hamster, some fish and a turtle, and they all had died of my curiosity. "Scarlet, a pet is what you need. It will soften your roughness." Daddy Laveau said. I loved my daddy. He was always giving me things to try and melt my rigid heart. I just wasn't that easily moved by life or the things that occupied it. I did not want to disappoint him and so I tried when I could, but the trying never lasted for too long. Something stirred in my soul when I did bad things, it was a good stir.

Momma Laveau said that I was just enlightened and curious. "You should not worry over Scarlet so much. She was just born to walk a different path," My momma had said to my daddy. She told me that I was on a path that would lead me to things that most people would never know or believe existed. Momma Laveau told me that I was the lucky kind that had been born with a veil over my face. She said that it was a family heirloom and that her and my grandfather had also been born with the same type of veil. That was the reason that my momma always found understanding in my peculiar ways and chose to keep me close.

I was excited when Daddy Laveau gave me that kitten for my birthday. I looked at her orange stripes and called her Tiger. I loved having things that belonged to me only, something that I could do anything I wanted with. But Tiger turned out to be a pest and not as obedient as I tried to make her. We never really got along. I remember the night Tiger insisted on purring and scratching in spite of my demands for her to stop.

"Do it again and I will skin you alive and make fur coats for my dolls," I hissed at Tiger.
She stood her ground staring at me through the moonlight filled bedroom full of ruffles and frills, dolls and toys. I admired her audacity but not enough to let her get away with being disrespectful and rude to her own master. It was a school night and I needed my rest and my due respect. Tiger continued to purr and scratch. "Stop it dammit!"

I hated that damn cat but did not want to break my daddy's heart by giving her back or losing her. I pulled my bedspread over my ears and tried to ignore her but Tiger would not stop and my rage got the best of me. "So you insist on irritating me, you little bitch," I said leaping from my bed to snatch Tiger's tiny little body up.

My first thought was to toss her out my bedroom window, but I knew she would just stand out there and cry to be let back in the house. I was so fed up with Tiger and I no longer wanted to clean up behind her or have to listen to her noise. To make things worse, she scratched up my favorite chair. Tiger had to go and she had to go that night.

I took a suitcase and a blanket from my closet all while holding Tiger by the neck, and she was scratching me and wailing. I prayed that my parents would not hear her and catch me before I could get rid of Tiger. Finally, I was able to get her wrapped up in the blanket and drown out her cries. I tossed the blanket in the suitcase, zipped it up and placed it back in the closet. *Good riddance, I can finally get some rest.*

The next morning I took Tiger out the suitcase and removed her limp body from the blanket. Her eyes were shut and her mouth was stretched open as if she had been gasping for air. I put my finger inside of her mouth to toy with her little sharp teeth. I held Tiger up and shook her a bit, she was good and dead. I smiled and placed her beneath my bed and headed to the kitchen for breakfast and homeschooling. *That was an easy fix.*

After breakfast Momma Laveau put down a bowl of milk for kitten.

"Scarlet, let Tiger out of the room." She said while smoothing the side of her tightly pinned back hair.

I moved from the table slowly, but not too slow as to bring attention to myself. Just slow enough to be my defiant self. It was my way mostly. I approached my room and called for Tiger and of course there was no answer.

"Tiger get your butt out here now and drink your milk." I yelled to nothing but the memory of a mischievous cat. I crawled on my bare scratched knees to the right side of my bed and lifted the pink and white stripped bed skirt. I inhaled before breathing out and then screaming.

"MOMMY! TIGER WON'T WAKE UP, COME QUICK!"

Momma Laveau rushed to my side with Daddy Laveau in toe. She swooped me up in her arms and my daddy reached beneath the bed to pull Tiger out. He held her for a minute checking her out. Daddy looked to momma and shook his head. "I am sorry," he said to the both of us as he left my room. I pretended to sob as my mother comforted me and tried to convince me that Tiger was in heaven. Daddy Laveau soon joined us and told me that everything would be okay. He said that maybe Tiger was sick when he bought her and then promised me a new kitten soon.

"But daddy, I don't want to replace Tiger."

"That's okay Scarlet. Nobody is going to force you to do anything that you do not want to." Daddy Laveau said while taking me into his loving embrace.

Momma Laveau canceled homeschooling that day and Daddy Laveau called out from work. We spent the day as a family. My parents wanted to make sure that I was okay and reinforce the love that they had for me. When they thought I was sleeping later that evening, I heard Momma Laveau and Daddy Laveau talking.

"Samson, do you think Scarlet will be okay, did we do enough to soothe her today?"

"Yes Victoria, we did all that we could. Let us just pray that we did not miss anything."

"What do you mean?"

"I am sure you know the answer to that."

Part 1

Chapter One
Scarlet

The ways of a woman was something that only God and I could comprehend. It was a good damn thing that I knew Koral's intentions or I would have done away with her a long time ago. One thing I despised was a delayed person and Koral was always late. I made my usual threat while waiting on her to arrive for her session. *This will be her last reading, and just maybe I'll make something up to scare the hell out of her.* I paced my wooden floors wearing the fresh shine down to calm my nerves a bit. I kept looking out the window for Koral and cursing her name at the same time. *This little bitch had better hurry up. As if I don't have better shit to do than wait on her trifling ass.* No way was I going to spend my day waiting around on an insensitive woman. I had waited long enough. I decided to write a note and place it on my front door. A note stating that I was unavailable for the remainder of that day.

It started to rain heavily as I prepared the letter. I ran to close my windows to keep the rain out of the house and off of my recently waxed floors. It was then that I spotted the infamous Koral in the distance. The inconsiderate heifer was running down the street toward my house screaming for me to open the door. I took my time about the door for I was in no hurry. Once I reached it, I stood patiently behind the screen door with my arms crossed and my face visibly upset. Koral stood drenched with pouted lips and a wet brown bag.

"Bonjour Mes Amis. I have Champagne and strawberries for you." She said in a baby's voice.

I rolled my eyes. "Maybe I do not want any Champagne. What else do you have?"

"Come on Scarlet! The bus ran late and I wanted to get us something to drink." Koral batted her thick lashes over pleading eyes. "I thought we could make a Marie Laveau. Do you have any more of that raspberry liqueur?" She continued.

"Marie Laveau huh." Koral knew how much I enjoyed those and I did have some raspberry liqueur in the cabinet.

"Shit girl. You know how I hate to wait. Now I doubt if you will get a reading today. I do have other people to see besides Koral Baptiste."

"I'm really sorry and I do not care about my reading, we can do it another day Scarlet. Now, can I please come in?'

"I guess you can." I said as I unlatched the screen door and turned to walk away.

"Merci Beaucoup."

The door slammed shut behind Koral. She stood biting on her lower lip while dripping wet on my newly waxed floor. *Better be damn glad that you are my best friend.* Sometimes I wanted to kill Koral, but most days I loved her to death. We had been close since early childhood. Koral's grandmother, better known as Nana to all, had raised Koral from an infant Even though Koral was now twenty-four, Nana was still raising her in some ways. Koral's birth mother, Precious Baptiste, had run off to join an anonymous dance company in New York. Precious had never come back for Koral nor attempted to call or write for her. I told Koral long ago that there was no sense in ever trying to find her mother because she was dead. Koral believed me, she knew I had the gift of sight and therefore she never tried to find her mother, but that did not stop her for wanting me to find out just how Precious had died. As for Koral's birth father, he could have been any dark-skinned man walking the streets of New Orleans. That is what Nana had told her and the reason she was much darker than Precious and Nana. Nana had been like my own grandmother for many years. Their old shabby Camelback house used to be right behind my own and had served as a second home. A few years ago Nana's house had started to rot and she and Koral were forced to move out after the city condemned it. We now had to take to the bus or a cab when we wanted to spend time together.

"I just waxed my floor." I said while handing Koral a towel.
"Thanks Scarlet."
"Umm hmm. Don't mention it."

I sat and watched Koral undress. She kept eyeballing me as she pulled the long sundress down from her slender body and allowed it to fall. I laughed and stared on as she struggled with her old fashioned bra. Her breast were much too pretty for that old tan thing. They were full and perfectly brown with huge nipples that seemed to be saluting me. I was enjoying the show when Koral stopped to stare back at me batting her long curly lashes. She shyly wrapped her long and well defined arms around her breast.

"What?" I said.
"Are you enjoying yourself Ms. Laveau?"
"I am and so are you. So continue."
"Will you help me?"
"I had every intention to do so." I said walking toward her.
"Lucky me."

Koral smelled of fresh rain and jasmine. I removed her arms from her breast and traced the drops of rain with the tip of my finger. She was so dark and lovely. Her high arched eyebrows were sort of a welcoming sign over her slanted glossy eyes. She had these voluptuous lips that lay beneath her stretched nose. Koral reminded me of one of those exotic cats, dangerously beautiful.

We had been intimate for years but never a couple. It had always been just good sex between friends. I played with a handful of Koral's short curls with one hand while tracing circles around her nipples with the other. Her chest moved up and down as she sighed deeply. It was her way of letting me know that she wanted more. I grabbed her thick lips with mine and made love to her mouth as my nails explored the arch in her back. Koral's womanly scent magnified. Only now it mixed in with a hint of soft musk. I laid my head between her breasts and listened to her heart beat anxiously for me. I fell to my knees and looked up into her eyes.

"Please." She whispered.

I placed my hand between her legs and massaged her lips. Her panties were already wet from the rain and now soaked from expectation.

"Tell me what you want?" I said.
"You're the fortuneteller. Why don't you read my pussy."

I placed my hand inside of Koral's panties to play with her protruding clit.

"She wants to be sucked." I informed, while undressing her.
"I agree." Koral said as she opened her legs wider and lay back against the wall to invite me to dine at her temple.

We spent half of the day pleasing each other between glasses of Champagne and heavy rain showers. It felt so good having a friend you could count on when the rest of the world betrayed you. She was more than my best friend; she was my secret keeper and sometimes lover. I knew that I would always have Koral Baptiste in my life no matter what. She was my faithful companion and I would always be available to her, heart and soul.

When we finished our random love session, Koral and I shared a hot bath and a joint. We both loved getting high and marijuana was a safe high. It was one of our favorite pastimes. Ever since we were young girls we had taken baths together. It was our way of connecting and sharing as one. We would talk about any and everything. I would mostly talk and Koral would mostly listen. She and I did not have any secrets between us. I trusted her with my life and she trusted me with her everything. I lay between her soft and lengthy legs in the hot soapy water and confessed all of my desires.

"Koral, have you ever thought about killing somebody?"

Koral gasped a little before answering. "How many times are you going to ask me that? My answer is still no! Do you want someone dead or something?"

"Naw, not anyone in particular anyhow."

"What is going on in that devious little head of yours Scarlet?"

"Nothing really, just wondering if we could get away with murder is all."

" *'We?'* Is all?"

Koral stiffened a bit. My intentions were not to frighten her but if I could not share something that was eating away at me with my best friend, then I was not in need of one. I had tried on numerous occasions to speak with Koral about this thing that just kept gnawing at me. It was a persistent thought that I could not rid my mind nor heart of.

"As in *us*." I said as I tilted my head back to look up into Koral's eyes and place the joint between her lips.

"I'm sure *we* could. Too bad *we* don't have anyone that *we* would want to kill huh?" Koral said with a wicked laugh.

"I'm thoughtful." I replied as I stood up to exit the tub. The water was getting cold and Koral had jokes.

I grabbed my robe to cover myself. "Well if I ever needed to kill someone, would you help me?"

Koral sat silent for only a second. Her eyes pleaded with mine but I refused to back down. I needed to know.

"Of course I would Scarlet. I'd die for you." She finally answered.

I was not surprised but filled with pride that I had the most valuable friend in the world.

"And I you Koral."

I kneeled beside the tub and removed the half moon and sun pendant and necklace from my neck. I smiled and dangled it in front of Koral's bright eyes. She smiled wide and made joyful sounds as she sat up in the tub to allow me to place the necklace around her neck. I kissed her on the shoulder several times.

Koral looked to me with tear filled eyes. She was always such an emotional mess of a woman.

I chuckled a bit. "What's mine is yours." I said.

Chapter Two
Koral

Scarlet stood in front of a full length cherry wood antique mirror. It was a little worn, but the floral carvings were just as beautiful as the reflection it held. Scarlet released her natural red locs from an up do and allowed them to fall around her waist. I watched her as she liked to be watched. She led my eyes in the direction of her choice as she swayed like a snake in front of the mirror while teasing with her lip piercing. She had a red splash of a birthmark on her right inner thigh that begged for my attention as well. I knew not to move myself from the tub until Scarlet was done with her seductive performance.

She had a natural way of being commanding even in her silence. I loved the way that she sort of bossed my heart around. I would do anything to have her as my own, but Scarlet had said that she was not a lesbian. She claimed that her soul was not bound to one world or another. She was not promised to one single soul and she was free to love whomever she pleased, whenever she wanted to without need to answer anyone.

At times I grew envious of how Scarlet was able to love more than one person at the same time while my heart belonged to her only. She had even paraded her lovers in front of me without ever thinking of the damage it did to my heart. I put up with Scarlet for many reasons and all were solid reasons. Scarlet knew things. She could read me and of that she took advantage. She had always known my thoughts and my path in life.

Ever since we were little girls running up and down the streets barefoot, she had known every single thing about me. So it angered me when she pretended to not know or not care that my heart longed for her like a motherless child in search of validation. I never stayed angry though because Scarlet was also very honest with me and so I stayed faithful in love with her because I chose to be a fool for love.

Scarlet proceeded to rub strawberry gloss across her perfect little lips while watching me from the mirror. I hated when she read me without my permission, it was a rude thing to do. I had to think of something else quick before I angered her with my thoughts.

"Scarlet?"

"Koral?"

"Please don't."

"Then stop musing over things in which you have no control."

"I am only thinking of our love making."

Scarlet threw the gloss down into the sink and walked toward me. Her silk leopard printed robe was wide open as she approached me angrily. I could gawk at her flawless body for forever.

"Do not insult me Koral. Or I will come in the night and steal your breath away from that delicious body of yours."

"No need for threats Scarlet Rose Laveau." I said backing down.

Her eyes were flushed and bitter. I knew then that I had gone too far. How I wished I could have better controlled myself but it was too late.

"Then I will not tolerate your lies! Now get dressed and get out." Scarlet demanded.

Once I finished dressing. I found Scarlet sitting naked at her reading table. She was just as content as could be. Her locs hung across her shoulders exposing the flamed rose tattoo on the upper right side of her back. I stood behind her admiring the rose and another tattoo that I had loved on many times before. The other tattoo was right above her waistline, it was a black tribal like

Veve symbol. Scarlet had told me that it represented a passage way from the physical to the spiritual world. I pushed the thought of my tongue tracing the tattoos out of my head and approached her with caution.

"Scarlet, I'm sorry for messing up our evening. Is there anything that I can do to fix it?" I whined.

She never turned to look at me. She kept busy placing the tarot cards on the table before her.
"

Don't fret Koral. I forgive you as always my love. But I want you to go home and tend to Nana. She needs you now, you know?"

"Yes, I suppose so." I said and turned to leave.

As I stepped down from Scarlet's porch I stood a moment looking over her wildflower infested yard. I heard Scarlet call after me. I turned to greet her nude body standing right behind her screen door. I turned to see if anyone else was looking in our direction.

"Best friend?"

"Oui?" I said all too eager and assuming that she would ask me to stay.

"Come to me for a minute." Scarlet ordered.

I went to her like the obedient servant that I had been for so many years.

I stood trying to cover her nudity from any on looking neighbors, though Scarlet could give less than a damn about them. She opened the door and my eyes went immediately down to her slight red haired covered vagina, the same naturally red hair that covered her head and narrow eyebrows. I stood like a kid waiting for my gift, because anything that she offered would be one.

"We should go down to Bourbon Street and listen to some Jazz soon, yes?" Scarlet said with a half smirk.

I smiled at her so called apology. It was the only way she knew how to apologize for being so stern with me. Though she would not take back her demand for me to return home and that is what I really wanted. Instead she offered me a night out on the town and that gave me something to look forward to. I always enjoyed our outings and Scarlet always made sure that I had a good time. She leaned forward pressing her bare and small breast up against me and then placed my face to hers for a goodbye kiss. I lingered at her silky and soft lips for as long as she would allow. Scarlet pulled away and placed her forehead on my chest. She placed small kisses between my breasts and whispered very lightly, "Goodbye for now."

I strolled in the fading daylight thinking about Scarlet and wondering how long it would take the bus to come. It was supposed to arrive every hour on the hour, but it seemed to come when it felt like it. I stood at the bus stop with my back up against a rusted and slanted stop sign.

The bus finally arrived a half hour late and before I could get on good, some guy damn near knocked me down to get off.

"Watch it!" I screamed in his direction.
He looked back and spat on the ground. "Bitch!" He screamed back and ran off down the street in an obvious hurry.

He almost knocked me down and yet he still felt the need to curse at me for saying something. I shook my head and boarded the bus. As the bus passed Scarlet's house I noticed the rude guy opening her gate. Maybe he was going to get a reading and just maybe he was going to love on the woman that I loved. I hated the thought of that but I just never knew with Scarlet. She wouldn't stand for me asking about it either. Not that we could not talk about any and everything but because she would sense my resentment and accusations. I never wanted to anger her on purpose so I chose my battles with her wisely. I felt a little jealous and sulked in my anger the entire fifteen minute ride home. I hated that I loved Scarlet so much at times, but nothing or anyone could ever change that.

Chapter Three
Scarlet

I really despised the way people pounded on my door as if I was hard of hearing. I decided to dress slowly and allow the Negro to knock for awhile. It was a little warm in my house and the window fans were only putting out more heat. The icebox was my only means to cool off temporarily. After I pulled on a tube dress, I stood with the freezer door open and allowed the coolness to soothe me. My visitor kept at knocking with such urgency that you would have thought someone was after him. Jessie French was a friend of a friend. He had called earlier that day requesting a reading. He said it was urgent and offered to pay double to have same day service if I would agree to see him. Money was always a voice of reason when I had to make a decision. I took a banana popsicle from the freezer and tore it open as I headed toward my impatient customer. I swung the front door open in response to being annoyed by the persistent knocker.

"Mr. French, I assume." I said while sucking on my popsicle as if it were the head of a penis. I so enjoyed torturing men. He could barely answer me.
"Ye…yes. You can call me Jessie. And you are Ms.Scarlet?" He said standing as tall as the doorframe.
I took my tongue and circled around my popsicle before sliding it in and out of my mouth again and smiled slyly at his reddened and rounded boyish face.

"Ms. Laveau to you, after all, you are a stranger sir. And it is the polite thing to do when greeting someone you know nothing about," I advised him while catching the flow of banana juice from my bottom lip.

"I apologize truly Ms. Laveau. I meant you no harm. I only want some answers to my problems if you will."

I laughed aloud and permitted the pathetic man into my home. He would be an easy read. His thoughts were in his pants at that moment and he would surely forget half of the questions that he had attempted to memorize.

"Place the payment in the dish beside you and give me your hand." I demanded while tossing the popsicle stick into a nearby trashcan.

He did as I said while pushing a falling cigarette back in place behind his big ear.

"Since I don't know you that well, I will need you to place your hands atop of mine to get a perfect reading. If you become a regular, I will eventually be able to read you with accuracy from a mile away."

"If you give me the answers I need, I will be back again Ms. Laveau."

"It may not be what you need but it will be the truth Mr. French. Now shall we begin?"

"Yes," he answered while biting on a hung nail.

I bowed my head and received Jessie's truth and gave thanks in my spirit's native tongue.

"This woman that you will ask to marry you, she is a good woman and will be faithful to you all of her days. She will bare you a son and name him for you."

The stranger smiled all too swiftly while leaning back in the chair. Before he could thank me I wiped the smile from his face permanently.

"Her days are numbered. She only has two years of herself to give to you."

"What do you say, Ms. Laveau?"

"I'm saying that she will die shortly after your second anniversary and you will be a single father."

Jessie French looked to me for understanding. I could hear his heart pick up and his spirit lie down.

"Do you know the reason?" He asked with tears clouding his rich brown eyes.

"From the virus that you carry in your body Sir."

His eyes frowned with his big chapped mouth as his fist pounded the table.

"I don't have any fucking virus woman."

"Please do not curse me. You asked for my help and I'm telling you what I know."

"Blasphemy. You are the fucking devil and I rebuke you in the name of the Heavenly Father."

"Laissez!"

"What?"

"Get the fuck out!"

Mr. French ran up out of my home as if it were an inferno. People only wanted to accept what they wanted to hear and the truth did not work like that. I was used to both angry and satisfied patrons from every Parrish in the Big Easy. It all came with the territory. I just did not understand fighting against the truth. Mr. French accepting it and taking precautions would have been the manly thing to do. I looked after him knowing that his days were numbered as well and also knew that I would never be able to let him know.

It started to rain again and being shut up in my hot house was the last place I wanted to be. I walked out in the rain and allowed it to stroke and comfort my body and soul. Tears from heaven were always a refreshing thing.

Chapter Four
Koral

Nana stood over the kitchen sink with her bent back toward me as I entered the house. I took a seat at our small and round wooden table which only had two chairs, one for me and one for my Nana. We did not have much but we had each other and that was plenty. I reached down to remove my ballet styled flats from my aching feet.

"Been with that nasty gal again, oui?"

"You know her name Nana and she used to be one of your favorites."

"She was never no nothing of mine gal. I love them people of hers. Has nothing to do with her and everything to do with the way I treat her."

I leaned my head back to rest against the chair and rub my temples. My Nana was half of my world and Scarlet was the other half. I would be nothing without them and love would only be a word with no meaning. I decided to try and change the subject. The last thing I wanted to hear was a bunch of negative remarks about Scarlet. She had her different ways and all, but that is what made her special in my eyes.

"Nana what are you doing up? You should be resting and I told you I would do the laundry tomorrow. Why do you insist on washing things out with your hands when there is no good reason to do so?"

"Gal, speak what you know, these here are precious things, much like you. I wash them in this here Woolite to preserve the beauty of them. You put them in some manmade machine and you ruin them for good. Besides, give me something to do, stead of worrying over you all the time." Nana said with a wave of her hand.

I went over to my grandmother and placed my hands on her tired shoulders. I tried to rub some of that unnecessary concern for me out of them. Last thing I wanted was her stressing over me. I was a woman well into my twenties and able to make decisions for myself. Nana had been a good second mother, but I was full and grown. It was due time that I cared for her. I stood behind her small and fragile but determined brick colored frame watching her bony hands and rock-hard knuckles fuss over the few delicate pieces of clothing that we owned. They were her prized possessions and she treated them much like she treated me.

"Let me finish those for you. Why don't you rest now Nana."

"I'll rest when I am good and dead. You need to find a better man and some new friends. It's just unnatural the way you hang on that gal every minute."

"Now Nana, you know as well as I do that Scarlet is my best friend and that she cares for me just as much as I care for her. Now stop it already and get some rest. Want me to fix you something to eat?"

"I want you to get some damn sense in your head and see that gal for what she is. She ain't nothing from God! Ain't her folks fault either, them good people."

I closed my eyes and scratched the back of my head hoping that Nana's lecture would be over soon. "Now Nana."

"Do not 'Now Nana' me. Sometimes you just get stuck with what you get. Her evil ways the real reason they ran off to Florida and left her here."

"Nana! You should be ashamed of yourself. There is no truth to that. The Laveau's retired to Florida and asked Scarlet to go along with them. She wanted to stay here."

"And her folks wanted her to stay." Nana said shaking her head.

"Now you know how much they love Scarlet. I won't listen to anymore of this."

"You can hear me now or wish like holy hell you would've heard me later gal."

My grandmother continued to hand wash the garments as I turned and left the small kitchen that smelled of Woolite and day old fried chicken. There was no good reason to heed anything she had spoken against Scarlet. Scarlet had always been there. She made sacrifices and all for me and Nana. She had even given up her savings to help us move into a safer house when ours was condemned by the city. Maybe my Nana could ignore all of that and call Scarlet evil but I knew it was nothing but genuine love with no price tags.

I sat on the edge of my full sized quilted bed and undressed. My thoughts were with all of that love Scarlet and I had made earlier. I wished that I could be sleeping with her every night. I would embrace that creamy skin of hers and fondle her fire red locs all night long. Her smell lingered on me even after our bath and just maybe I had purposely left some of it on me. I licked my lips to try and recapture the moment while teasing my insides. I wondered what Scarlet was doing at that moment and if she thought of me while lying in bed as well. It didn't matter though; I knew I owned at least a piece of her heart and mind. One day soon she would see that we belonged together and Nana would have to realize it too. God forbid if I had to choose between the two of them. Because I honestly do not know if I could ever choose need over desire.

Early the next morning I arranged Nana's homegrown vegetables and freshly baked goods into a shopping cart. I stuffed a wooden box that contained her handmade jewelry down the side of it. It was time to head out to the corner of our street and set up shop for the day's earnings. Nana had been a peddler all of her life. We made enough to survive and would have made more if Nana would charge what her stuff was really worth. It did no good to argue with her about charging her neighbors more than what she felt they could afford. Nana said that they were in the same sinking boat that we lived on. I had taken over the roadside business after Nana got sick. She was mostly confined to the house now. Nana still grew the vegetables, baked the goods and crafted the jewelry. Only now I was in charge of selling them.

"Nana I'm out. See you this evening."

"Make sure you put on some sunblock; do not need to be no darker!" She yelled back.

"Love you too Nana."

I sat next to the food stand beneath my big straw hat that shielded me from the sun. I had to fan away the heat and the flies the same. It was so damn hot that day. I sat praying for rain to fall and cool me off. Maybe I could have called upon Scarlet and asked her to do a rain dance, something I would have certainly loved to watch. Scarlet had real magic, she could make the rain fall and the sun shine and my heart beat a million times a minute.

Just as I was sitting there reminiscing about Scarlet, I noticed that my view was now shaded. I stood to welcome my customer only to discover that it was my boyfriend Pierre DePaul. He was a very striking guy. Most folks said that he was much too pretty to be a man. Surely God had denied some woman her right to be beautiful. Paul is what I called him because Pierre only added to his prissiness. He was tall as a tree with a slight muscular build to his thin frame. He had this natural glow that traveled from his lovely face to the tip of his pedicured toes. Paul could certainly pass for white, especially at first glance. You had to stare in his face for more than a few minutes to find his Negro. His hair was straight as straw and silky black with a slight bend on the ends. He had lips as thin as paper that disappeared between my two big ones when we kissed. Paul said that he loved being smothered by my lips. His eyes were as green as fresh cut spring grass and he walked with a purpose. Paul was a really good man. He wanted to marry me and move far away from New Orleans. Only I would never leave my Nana or Scarlet and he did not want to take them with us. He assumed Nana would try and rule his house and that Scarlet would turn him into a frog. So he said he was waiting around long enough for me to get some sense in my head. I guess he would be waiting forever.

"What does a man have to do to spend some time with his woman?"

"Stalk her on her job I guess." I said with as much sarcasm as I could muster up.

"I reckon so Ms. Koral. While I'm stalking you I may as well get that kiss I have been waiting on."

I quickly pecked Paul on the lips and stepped away from him.

"That is no way to kiss your man, woman!" Paul said and pulled me back in for a deeper kiss. I let him have his way for a second and then pulled away.

"Now Paul, you know Nana will have a fit if one of these old ass gossiping hens go back and tell her that I was making out during business hours."

"I just can't help myself; you are always looking so damn scrumptious Koral."

It felt good hearing that I was beautiful. I know Nana did not really mean anything by always cautioning me to stay out of the sun, but it did make me self-conscious about being so much darker than the people I loved. Both Scarlet and Paul admired my darker skin and I think I would have felt much better about it had I known where it came from. I found myself staring at every dark skinned man in New Orleans wondering if he could be my daddy.

Paul's lips were just a moving and I was sitting there daydreaming about nonsense.

"You will just have to get a hold of yourself Paul."

"I just wanted to walk right up to you and take a bite out of those long shiny legs of yours. All I could think about is how they have embraced my soul so many times."

"Why Paul! This is not the time or the place to discuss such things." I chastised while looking around.

"I will be over tonight you hear? No excuses! And I have something for you."

"No excuses, but I do have plans to go down to Bourbon Street with Scarlet, so make it late as possible."

"Always Scarlet! I swear I believe you two be doing the do!" He said jokingly this time.

"Paul! Later okay?"

"Okay… mi amour."

Paul skipped away with a song in his heart. He had it bad for me and I liked him enough but I had it even worse for Scarlet. Paul hated Scarlet. He wanted nothing to do with the likes of her. He called her "voodoo bitch." Scarlet was always threatening to put a spell on Paul. She would tease him something awful and of course I was always caught in the middle of their drama. Paul was no threat to Scarlet and she only bullied him because she could. Now Scarlet was a big threat to Paul and he made sure to make it known as often as possible. He said that Scarlet was the kind of woman that stole from men what God intended them to have. He said that she was devils spun and meant our relationship no good. I had to remind him that Ms. Scarlet Rose Laveau was my best friend for life and the two of us would always be a package deal. He could take it or leave it.

Chapter Five
Scarlet

"Such a beautiful creature should never be alone." Some bold Negro said while standing behind me. If he had the guts to approach me, then I had the guts to play his male ego game.

"One, you never presuppose any such thing based on looks alone."

"I'm taking my chance Ms. Scarlet Laveau."

"So, you know who I am. Cute." I said while spinning around on the worn leather barstool.

Koral was late as usual and I had nothing better to do while waiting but to entertain a stranger. He was no different from the many men in New Orleans that I knew nothing about but they claimed to know much about me. Most of it was idle gossip from the local women that had known my mother or had come to me for a reading. Some of the talk was from folks spreading rumors passed down by other folks about what they thought they knew of me and mine.

"Why of course. You my darling are the cat's pajamas. Whispers go all through the club about who you be."

I crossed my bare legs after giving him a quick peek of my womanhood. It was surely exposed through the see through under garment that I had chosen to wear that night. He smiled as if it had been an invitation, big ol' white teeth against deep tinted dimpled skin. He was bald and handsome enough and wore a face and body strong and chiseled like a superhero. I sat there imagining his dark skin soaked atop my yellow body.

"And you would be?" I said extending my hand that he took in with a lingering kiss. I had to snatch it away to remind him that it was mine.

"Abdu Johnson, Madame."

"Another servant of God. Nice to meet you." I said with some sarcasm.

"A servant for life. Who else would protect us from such beautiful things?" Abdu continued to flirt.

I couldn't help but smile back, after licking my teeth to make sure no lipstick was on them. I searched Abdu from head to toe as he continued to pump up my head with things I always heard but in a more experienced way. He wore tan slacks and a white buttoned-down short sleeved shirt. I could see his swelled chest through the thin material. Abdu was the type of man that I would choose to bed to bring children into my world. But I knew early in life that my heart did not desire a husband and that it would be unjust to bring a child to life without one.

"Another drink or dance or possibly both?" Abdu asked while staring at the almost empty goblet of vodka behind me.

"Thank you kindly. But it's still early and I'm waiting on a friend."

"A male friend?" He inquired.

I smiled at his audacity. "A woman."

"Good!"

"She is good, very good actually. Much better than any man I have been with." I responded.

Abdu's yummy smile ran from his baffled face. I smirked as I jumped down from the stool and moved past him. I could feel him staring in my direction as I approached an apologizing Koral.

"Forgive me Scarlet."

"Never mind that Koral." I grabbed her by the arm and pulled her to the dance floor.

"Wait a minute." Koral protested. "I need a drink first."

"Not just yet. I will explain in a minute." I said as I pulled her close to me and whispered in her ear what had just taken place with Abdu.

Koral looked toward Abdu and we both laughed aloud while dancing as close as possible. I knew Abdu was burning up with envy as he sat on the barstool that I had once occupied. He stared at us while gulping down something in a glass.

"We should take him to my place and screw his brains out and then kill him." I laughed.

"How about we just let him watch us make out and then kill him?"

"Why let a good man go to waste?"

"Because I have a man." Koral bragged.

"Oh, is that what you call him?"

"Don't be mean Scarlet. I don't want to cheat on Paul is all."

I stared at Koral wondering what the hell she thought about us. "I guess fucking another woman is not considered cheating?"

Koral did not respond. She stood staring at me with saddened eyes. I knew what that look was about. She wanted nothing more than to be more than my lover. But I was never going to belong to anyone, not even Koral. And as much as I loved her, she could never own what I possessed. My appetite was fierce and something not of this world. I was not born to be slaved beneath a relationship. I wanted to love freely. Love had no face and love had no color and love was androgynous. Or maybe I was speaking of sex because my heart was a deep dark hole that I often searched for a feeling but there was nothing but space looking for more of that same feeling. A space big enough to hold whatever and whomever I wanted to occupy it. I would not let Koral or anyone else smother me with their expectations. If I could, I would give her anything in the world that her heart desired, anything but me.

"Let's get that drink." I said while walking away from Koral and towards the bar.

Abdu had left by the time we reached the bar. Koral and I took a seat and ordered drinks. We scanned the club for potential victims while ignoring the many men that approached us and joked about the jealous women that resented us. We got a few more dances in before Koral started pretending to be tired from working all day. I rolled my eyes because I knew she must have made plans with Paul but would never skip out on a night with me. It was her way of trying to please both us.

"Whenever you are ready to leave we can go. I am kind of beat from working in all that damn sun today."
"Let's go." I said heading out of the club.
"Are you sure? I'm not rushing you." Koral lied."
"It's cool. Maybe another time."
"Another time?"
"Have you forgotten why we are here Koral?" I said turning to face her.
"Oh… that. No, I have not."
"Good, because you gave me your word that you would help."
"I know, and I will when the time is right."

We walked over to the phone booth across the street and called for a cab. As we waited for our ride to arrive, I took the opportunity to flirt with my friend. Koral was gorgeous under the moonlight. I wanted to make love to her right then and there and I would not have cared who protested or wanted to watch. She sat down on the old white woodened bench that was seated on the curb of the street. Her red mini dress stretched barely across her crotch and her legs went for miles before ending at her feet dressed in four inch black pumps. I stood against the stop sign licking my lips while allowing my eyes to crawl all over her. There were no words between us. Our thoughts were loud and as clear as automobiles traveling down the street shining their spotlights on our naughty feelings. The cab slowly approached us before stopping.

"You ladies called for a cab?" The white cab man asked.

"We did." I answered while gathering myself and making my way into the cab.

"Where should I drop you two beauties?"

"We are going to two different spots. But you can drop her first." I said while giving directions.

I whispered in Koral's ear how we could probably easily take the cabbie home and kill him before he had a clue that trouble was brewing. We giggled and he smiled back at us like some old dirty man. He was actually sort of handsome in a weird way. I took in his bearded covered slim face. He looked as if he played in a band with the many tattoos that lined and circled his arms and neck. I stared at him in a seductive way every time I caught him eyeing me in the mirror. I played beneath Koral's dress too. I wanted to give him something extra. It was the least I could do for him. I could see it in his eyes that he was begging for a show. I did not do much. I was just rubbing on her thick thighs. I'm sure that the cabbie assumed I was doing more.

We pulled in front of Koral's house and she reached over for a hug. I squeezed her tight and kissed her on the cheek as she turned to land her velvety lips on mine. I took them in knowing that Paul would be going behind me. He was always getting my sloppy leftovers. I started to ask her to go home with me but I did not want the company in the morning.

"Goodnight Beautiful." I sung.

"Night Scarlet." Koral replied beaming. "By the way, I love that shirt. I have been admiring it all night but kept forgetting to mention it."

I looked down at the black lace blouse that I had gotten from the thrift store. "Do you?"

"Yes. It is just as stunning as you."

I started unbuttoning my blouse. Both the cabbie and Koral looked on, Koral with desire and the cabbie with disbelief.

"Here you are my lovely. It is yours."

"I love you Scarlet Laveau."

"I know my lady."

Koral took the blouse knowing to never deny a gift from me. She used to be so shy about me giving her things but over the years of growing up together, she quickly learned that I didn't take too kindly to people refusing gifts. It would be rude to turn down a freely giving hand. I gave the cabbie my address and we headed toward my little pink trimmed sky blue house.

I sat in the back of the cab in my bra and skirt feeling a little chilly.

"I adore your hair." The cabby flirted.

I grabbed my reddened locs from my shoulders and lap and pulled them behind my head before letting them fall at will.

"Thank you." I managed.

"What would I have to do to get your number pretty lady?"

"The name is Scarlet Laveau."

"Yes, I heard it from your friend girl. Well Scarlet Laveau, I am Phillip, but I prefer Philly. And I would love to take you out sometime if possible"

"Anything is possible Philly. How about tonight? Are you free now?"

"No. But I can be." He said with too much joy.

Philly was assuming that he had just scored an easy lay. And just maybe his guess would be accurate that night.

We pulled up to my modest home and parked out on the curb. Philly jumped out to open my door but I stepped out prematurely to refuse him the control. He followed me sniffing like a dog through my opened and slightly rusting fence. I never closed the gate when I left home. It was a sign to everyone that approached my house that I was watching. It was almost like a "I dare you to enter my shit." If I was at home I kept the gate closed to let the world know that I was encircled in my dwelling.

"Welcome to my home." I said to Philly as I stretched out my arms and did a three-sixty turn. It belonged to me now that my parents were living down in Florida. Not much had changed though. My childhood pictures were still in the same place that my mother had placed them. I thought about redecorating but I could not bear the thought of having to say goodbye to both my parents and their belongings. And besides, my parents had spent good money and care on the things that took up space in my home. I held out my hand in front of the sofa before me and Philly took a seat. He was looking all around with such curiosity as I walked through my home lighting my way by candles.

"Are your lights off or something?"
"No." I said with no further explanation. I rarely used electricity; it took away from my natural energy.
"I see. You have a unique home. Do you live alone?"
"That's none of your damn business." I replied returning from the kitchen with a smile and an open beer.

He smirked with a tilt of his head as he raised the beer bottle in my direction. Our eyes met and stayed glued as I read his soul. Philly wanted more than sex, he wanted my company and was genuinely interested in knowing more about me. That was certainly different for a man, especially when I had invited him into my home on the first night wearing only a bra for a shirt.

I walked over to my mother's vintage fireplace that was also a bar and a record player made of solid mahogany wood. It was one of the many things left to me that I treasured and what a beauty it was. Janis Joplin was still inside the record player from the last time I played it. I gave her another spin and joined Philly on the couch.

I crooned. "A woman left lonely will grow tired of waiting... she'll do crazy things, yeah,   on lonely occasions."
"An exotic songbird you are."
"What do you know about Janis Joplin?"
"That she died early from an overdose."
"People always remember the shitty stuff about a person's life. I want to be remembered by the things that I enjoyed doing."
"That would be nice and quite possible in a perfect world." Philly teased.

"Our world is what we decide that it should be. We have control over it all Philly."

"If you say so." He responded in a distant tone.

Something hurtful had grabbed him from the inside and in that moment he had disappeared spiritually. It would have been easy for me to take control of Philly's body in his absence. But I had no intentions on killing him. I didn't want to do it alone and I was counting on Koral to help me pull it off successfully if I ever decided that he was the one. For now, I was just as interested in him as he was in me. I smiled at him through the candlelit room admiring the way his forehead creased at his thoughts. The four lines that had formed made him look a bit more mature.

"A blowjob for your thoughts." I said while lying down in his jean covered lap.

Philly's current situation returned to him at an instance. He looked down at me with intensity and reached to fondle my naked stomach with his tattooed palm. I closed my eyes to enjoy the pondering of my flesh. Tiny butterflies gathered and fluttered beneath my skin and traveled down below my bellybutton. Philly's hand followed in sync. He knew just how to touch me. He kept moving his hands down until he reached my middle. I enjoyed the way his fingers felt between my skirt and nylon panties.

"Tell me about you Scarlet. Tell me everything."

It was almost as if he was begging and that did not fit his heavy metal appearance. Philly was a sheep in a wolf's shell. I reached to play in his full and dark beard, it tickled my dainty hand.

"What would you like to know?"

"Your thoughts. Your everything."

"There's not much to tell about me Philly. And no real reason for me to tell you. This is just a night. Not the first night of our future. Can you deal with that?"

Philly pulled me up enough to bend back my head and receive his kiss. It was smoky but nice. He pulled me onto his lap as we continued to kiss. He finally let go of my lips to catch a breath and to whisper in my ear.

"I want you."
"You have me."

I jumped from his lap and motioned for him to follow me. Philly stopped short of joining me in my parent's room and stared into the empty room that adjoined it. It was a ceremonial room with wooden floor boards. It was the magic circle in the middle of the floor and adorned with tea candles that caught his attention.

"What's that for?"

I started to just ignore Philly or tell him to concentrate on fucking me. But I knew that he came without fear and would be satisfied with the truth. I pointed into the ceremonial room and at the magic circle.

"Within the circle one can transcend the physical world and take the mind to a deeper and higher level of consciousness. It acts as a protection barrier from all Evil and unwanted Entities."

Philly turned to enter the room and I followed him without protest. He stepped over the tea candles and signaled me with his long and thick finger. I laughed but took his invitation.

"My plans were to do you in my parent's bed and pretend that you were my father but I like your idea better." I said.

Philly walked patiently toward me and started unzipping my skirt. It fell to the floor as his eyes roamed over my small and tight figure. His long hairy arms came around my back to undo the one loop that held my strapless bra up. The slight change in temperature from a ghostly presence that was obviously present in the room made my nipples hard and erect.

Philly slid down to the floor taking my panties with him. He laid his heavy gelled head on my vagina and hugged my ass. He seemed to be praying, I felt some sort of wetness that was not attached to anything and wondered if the man was crying or if it was just me showing my readiness.

Philly positioned me around his strong neck and dug into me with his tongue. When I had enough, I made him let me down and fell to my knees with my ass up in the air and my legs opened and ready for whatever. Philly turned into a beast and ripped his clothes from his body. I smiled back at him.

"I've been a bad girl." I said looking back at his hungry face.

He winked at me before taking his position in back of me. I felt my once empty body become full with one quick thrust and then many. I screamed out like a wounded animal as Philly ravished my body doggy style in a circle of protection. I cried out his name in pleasure and to build his ego as he dug deeper into my soul with his manhood.

"Do I still have to pay for the cab ride?" Is all I could manage as Philly continued fucking me.

"No fucking way." He quickly replied before placing his head between my legs to drink from my well.

Chapter Six
Koral

Scarlet's blouse sat on my pillow waiting for me to wrap up my soul in comfort for the night. I removed my clothes quickly and pulled it on without buttoning it. I wanted to pretend that I was in her arms and wrapped up with her smell. Everything about that woman haunted me and at times I wondered if she had cast some sort of spell on me or maybe had some sort of voodoo doll with my name on it. It just made no sense how rooted I was in this one woman who only desired a piece of me. Scarlet was my constant thought between taking care of Nana and being with Paul. I just couldn't shake her, and tonight of all nights I wanted to be lying next to her teasing the tips of my fingers. Instead I had plans to see Paul, and not that he was not decent enough, it was just the comparison of that brought me down when I knew the difference. *Scarlet Rose Laveau, you are driving me insane.*

I lay in my bed with nothing but Scarlet's blouse on, her scent was heavy and her spirit lingered with it. Just as my hand slid down between my thick thighs I heard a familiar but startling knock. It was Paul and he was peeping in like some sort of stalker desperate and horny. I let up the window and stepped back from the window. His long leg reached down to the floor with little effort.

"Don't knock so hard. You will wake Nana and she will have your head."

"I'm sorry baby. I'm just a lil anxious to get in between your chocolate thighs." Paul said all giddy.

He managed to bump his head while putting his other leg through the window and then tripped across his big feet onto the shaggy carpeted floor. *What an idiot.* My eyes rolled to the back of my head as I hurried over to make sure that my bedroom door was locked. The last thing I needed was for Nana to catch Paul in my bedroom at that ungodly hour or anytime of the day really. I would never live it down and everyone in the neighborhood would know that Nana had a loose granddaughter.

Paul started pulling off his clothes as if in a competition to do so first. He dropped his pants so fast that I imagined that they had to have been already opened. His shirt and his newsboy hat went flying across my room landing at will. He stood there by the still open window with the lights from the neighbor's house shinning on his tight and white briefs. I looked down at his matching knee length socks and covered my mouth to keep from laughing. There was absolutely nothing sexy about his wardrobe. But he was a sure thing still.

"What is so damn funny Koral?" Paul said with his appetite showing.

"Nothing Paul! But please take those god awful socks off."

He rolled his eyes to the side of his head and back and then reached for his socks pulling them from his unattractive feet. I then wished that I had kept quiet about the damn socks. I was just thankful that it was dark and I did not have to see them much. Paul's face was always my mission when we were together. It made me dream of little baby girls with perfect faces and gorgeous curls.

I wanted to be a mother, a good mother, something my mother failed to be for one reason or another. I had heard of many reasons but I never really knew the truth. It was a damn shame that she died before I could find out. Scarlet had told me of her death during one of our readings. I did know that she had plans to return to me and died at her attempt to escape whatever she had gotten caught up in. The world is such a funny place. People always looking for better when the best is right in front of them, you just gotta remove the blinders. I damn near forgot about Paul when I felt his arms wrap around my body.

"You are wearing the hell out of that shirt, you sexy little devil." Paul said.

I stood there in Paul's embrace and we swayed to his humming of some song that only he knew. Paul could sing really well and once had dreams of becoming a singer. He even had a group and they had been somewhat famous down in the French Quarters. But like most groups they didn't make it because everybody wanted to play the chief and there can only be one if success would follow. Paul claimed that he really gave up singing to chase me. He knew that there was no way that he could travel all over the place or stay out most late nights in the bars and still keep an eye on me. He even said that his greatest concern was not a man taking me away but more so Scarlet keeping us apart.

I turned to Paul as he still held on and laid my head on his shoulders. He sung a sweet song that he wrote just for me. It was soothing and body aching. It was some soul deep bluesy type of music. Paul's lungs were a fine tuned piano. He could literally hum me into submission if he so desired when singing.

"I'm gonna love you always because you are the only one that makes my heart forget to move on to the next beat." Paul moaned in my ear.

"Is that right Pierre DePaul?"

"That is right Koral Depaul!"

"Baptiste."

"Not for long my dark chocolate… not for long."

Paul slid his hands down my ass and cupped both ample sides all at once. He loved my bottom the most and then my legs and then my lips. He loved every part of me really and would show me more often if I allowed it to be so. As Paul laid me down to love me I imagined Scarlet. Little red Scarlet, she was so red all over. Paul was just pretty enough to imagine luscious and lengthy cherry locs dangling from his head. His green eyes shone through the night lights but I was still able to pretend that he was Scarlet because her scent overpowered his. I wrapped my legs around Paul's bare back and as he entered me. I pretended that Scarlet was wearing a strap and I held on to her to drain the love that I needed from her veins. I had a perfect piece of man between my legs and all I could think of was my Magic Queen. Maybe I could have it all somehow, a baby from Paul, love from Scarlet and understanding from Nana. Now that would just be perfect, just perfect.

I woke to an early Sunday morning intruding like only a thief knew how to. Paul had left sometime before the sun stood up. Our love making had been satisfying and needed. I still wore Scarlet's laced black blouse with her heavy scent attached that was now mixed with mine and Paul's. I massaged my perky nipples with one hand in remembrance of my lovers and allowed my free hand to play in my wavy snatch below. Right before deciding that I would please myself before leaving bed, I heard Nana out in her garden talking to her vegetables. She believed that they were alive and treated them with love. She said that the love she poured into the ground was the reason for such a beautiful crop. I leaped from bed at that moment and went to bathe and join her. I needed to wash Paul's smell away and to also douche any semen away that may have escaped before Paul could pull out. Nana would scold me if she had any idea that I had allowed Paul between my legs before a proper marriage. My mother's mistakes were enough to hold over my head like a weighted halo of hell.

After my bath, I walked into the kitchen and was greeted with a plate of hotcakes and a side of fresh pork sausages. They were my favorite and still rather warm. Nana must have come back in to fix breakfast after she discovered I was awake. There was fresh squeezed orange juice, syrup and butter sitting right next to my ample plate. I dug in with an urgency right after giving my thanks to the good Lord. I loved my Nana and she loved me. She may not have said it too often but she showed it in many ways, like with good home cooking.

As soon as breakfast was finished, I grabbed my garden hat and rushed to join Nana in her garden with the last of my hotcakes still being chewed.

"Good morning my favorite woman in the whole wide world."

Nana hesitated before looking up at me. "You sure bout' that? And don't talk with food in your mouth child." Nana said with her nose scrunched up.

"Why would you say such a foolish thing like that old woman? Of course I'm certain, above all things." I replied with hand on hip and a pouted lip.

"I see. Well I reckon I should be honored if that is the case. What are your plans for the day?"

"To work the garden with you and enjoy a quiet evening at home with my Nana."

"Don't fuss over me child. You best be after that piece of fellow of yours and see to it that he makes an honest woman of you. You hear what I'm saying?"

"I'm in no rush Nana, all in due time."

Nana sucked her teeth and looked up at me deeply while shielding her eyes from the beaming sun with her left hand. She searched me for truth before shaking her head and returning her attention to her garden.

"Why don't you ask Paul over for dinner, give'em some of your good cooking?"

"You don't even care for Paul like that Nana."

"Yeah but you do and he ain't the worst thing that could happen to you. He is a good color, has fine hair and hell, he actually loves you Koral. I don't needs to love him."

"What does color have to do with anything Nana?"

"Everything. May not be right, but everything. The darker you are the harder life will be unless you are born with a silver spoon attached to your behind."

"Well Nana, you just as white as any white folk I know and our life hasn't been easy ever."

Nana looked me over long and hard. She made me nervous when she did not blink well after the allotted time.

"Don't be foolish child. This here ain't no bad life. We done had it good. Never went a hungry day in your life. You have been spared the knowledge of a bad life."

I felt bad telling Nana that our life had been hard. She was my protector and had done a damn good job of it. I never wanted her to assume that I was ungrateful for her raising me when she could have had less worries without having another mouth to feed. After all, she had raised her daughter already. It was my mother that had been selfish and left me on my Nana.

"You're right Nana. You have fed me well, mentally, physically and spiritually. I wouldn't change the life I have had and have with you for any other life. I love you so   much. Forgive me for being a prude."

"There's ain't nothing to forgive." Nana said while smiling. I kneeled down into the cool of the earth beside my worn and wrinkled but strong and determined Nana. *What would I ever do without you?*

Nana was planting a root garden. The summer season would soon be over and the cool weather would be rushing in without apology. We planted carrots, beets and parsnips, radishes, turnips, and rutabagas. It seemed as if we spent the entire morning planting vegetables and talking about life. Nana used our garden time to sow not only vegetables but wisdom. She wanted to caution me about all the bad things of life in hopes of sparing me some unnecessary suffering. I half listened because I knew that my Nana was speaking with a mother's heart and that her love for me blinded her from the walls that she would force me to put up in fear of life itself if I took in all that she offered.

There was a lot to learn from my Nana and I soaked up many things that she said. I always remembered to treat people as I wanted to be treated and was careful to not make enemies. Nana said to always greet with a smile, no matter what expression the next person was wearing. She said that life was a gift and we should always treat it as such. She made me promise to never take one ounce of breath for granted. I took heed to all of that and most things that my Nana told me. It was the other things she said that I did not listen to, like staying out of the sun and not getting any darker than I already was. I knew that she said it out of pure love and that she meant me no harm, but I enjoyed my darker complexion and received many compliments on it. I knew that my skin tone was not holding me back. It would kill Nana to know that she was my one reason for settling for less than I could have out of life. I was afraid for her and to leave her alone. I felt as if I owed her my everything, to make sure that she was okay now that I was the only one that could work and bring in the money. My Nana's well being meant the world to me and I planned to be there for her like she had been there for me and no sacrifice was too great. The world had nothing greater to offer me than what I had with Nana and Scarlet right there in Crescent City.

"Nana, you know I love you right?"

Nana looked to me and shook her head again. "Worry yourself none about this old bag of bones gal."

"Well I do and I am always going to be here for you."

"You hungry? I'm hungry." She said and got up from the ground brushing off the excess dirt from her hands and knees.

Nana left without really answering me but I knew that she was aware. I smiled at her and continued to work. Nana went to get lemonade and some tuna sandwiches for us to survive on until the garden was finished. I stayed on in the garden to finish up a row of carrots until she came out to setup lunch on our little picnic table. It was a much needed break. We had finished most of everything but the rutabagas. They would be the last thing to plant after lunch. I washed up at the water hose and joined Nana at the table.

Nana and I sat quiet for a moment enjoying the coolness of the lemonade and looking over our little garden. We put a lot of sweat in that ground. I sometimes worried over Nana doing so much, but she wouldn't stop if I demanded her to. She would work herself into a grave before sitting down and resting. That woman lived for harvest time. Nana would smile when she pulled up her crop of vegetables. She would call me out and tell me that it was time to reap what had been sown. She would hold up those big beautiful carrots after washing them and tell me how when you put love into something you got nothing but love back. But I had to wonder how true that was. I knew Nana had to have been a loving mother to my mother and yet she up and deserted me and Nana out of the blue one day. Precious Baptiste had told Nana that her dreams were calling for her and that she had to answer to them before it was too late to do anything about them. She said that she did not want to end up like Nana, worthless and old before her time. She kissed me bye (from what my Nana told me) and promised that she would send for us when she made it big.

Precious Baptiste wanted to be a showgirl and dance on Broadway. Nana said my momma had been a natural talent when it came to singing and dancing. She and my granddaddy spent every extra penny that they had on dance classes for her. They always knew that my momma was something special and that is why they had named her Precious. Precious Baptiste was a beautiful light skinned woman with long dark curls. She had eyes that begged you to do her heart's desire and a body to match. Nana said that is where I got my shapely body from and my momma got it from her daddy's side of the family. The women on that side were plentiful in the right places.

Nana was mostly white and shaped in a white way too, just as flat as a pancake with no hips, buttocks or curves to claim. That didn't matter to my Grandpa Samuel. He thought Nana was a great catch and one that could pass for white if she wanted to. He hurried up and married her and then turned around and hurried up and died after only giving her four years of marriage and one child. My momma was only three when her daddy died but Nana said that my momma never forgot her daddy. He died of complications of polio and Nana never did see it fit to marry again. She was still in love with a ghost of a man after all these years. She kept grandpa and my mother's pictures up all over the house. It was like living in a museum of the dead.

We finished up the rutabagas and headed in the house. I went to run Nana some bath water while she undressed. I had to wait my turn because we only had the one bathroom to share. While I waited I worked on a few pieces of Nana's homemade beaded jewelry. It was really popular in New Orleans. A lot of folks would come around the vegetable stand to buy Nana's jewelry. And as popular as it was Nana had still refused to charge what it was worth. Even if she charged for the labor she put into it we would make a lot more off that jewelry. She actually hand painted the beads and put in such fine and distinctive details. Her unique designs are what set it apart from other jewelry that was sold out on the corners. It was almost like her signature and I knew every piece of jewelry that belonged to her in that town being worn by many. The one I was finishing up had a bit of a vintage flare. The beads were sage and emerald in color and had a large antique brass heart with an etched swirl design to it. Nana put her heart and soul into everything she did. I wanted to desperately find a way to give her back some of what her sweat and blood was worth. I did not want my Nan's life to be in vain like my mother's had been. I would find a way to make things right for her, even if I had to die trying.

Chapter Seven
Scarlet

I woke with a throb near my pelvic area. I assumed that I had slept in a bad position and that the pain would eventually leave my body once I took a warm shower. But the sting was persistent and followed me through late afternoon. It was time to rid myself of that affliction. I sat in a quiet place to focus on the pain in my body. As I stilled my soul I looked through a nearby window up at a brilliant blue sky. It drew me right into its center and opened my head. I cleared my mind of everything and held the amethyst rock in my right hand nearest the pain in my body. I imagined the bright light from the sun filling my body from head to toe. The energy of it was stimulating and energizing.

"Bright light, shining light, heal my hurts with all thy might," I chanted repeatedly as the light moved through my body.

I allowed the light to expand outside of my head before concentrating and pushing all of my energy toward the source of agony.

"So let it be." I felt the pain crawl away as if it had been a black widow attached to my body and now heeding my command to flee.

I stood up and walked slowly to the living area and kneeled on the sofa to stare out the window and nothing but memories of my parents chasing me around that very front yard that was in front of me flooded my thoughts.

Some days I longed for my parents' presence. It had been almost a year since I last saw them. Daddy and Momma Laveau spoiled me to pieces and I enjoyed it so. They were always sending me things from Florida. We did not visit often but we found the time to talk at least once a week. I found myself wishing that I was lounging on the sofa between the two of them watching one of Daddy Laveau's westerns that he loved so much. I hated those cowboy movies but daddy never knew it. Anywhere that Daddy Laveau would be you would surely find my momma. She stayed attached to him as if her life depended on it.

Momma Laveau viewed my daddy as her guardian after her own father disowned her. Daddy Laveau promised that he would never leave her side and that he would do everything in his power to make up for her loss. My daddy kept his word.

Momma Laveau asked Daddy Laveau to move her near the beach to live out eternity after he retired. Daddy up and moved her to Florida just like that. They live in a cottage right off the beach. You can literally smell the salt as you pull into their neighborhood.

As much as I enjoyed visiting them I could never leave New Orleans behind. The Big Easy was my home and always would be. My daddy convinced my momma to stop nagging me about moving down to Florida. He told her that I was an adult and allowed to live where I wanted to. Momma Laveau finally loosed her reigns and gave me her blessing to stay. I knew that she worried over me and the things that I was capable of doing. She just didn't understand that I had a storm brewing in me. Nothing could drive it away but allowing that storm to take place.

I decided to call my parents before continuing my day. I swear they allowed their phone to ring too many times before deciding to pick up.

"Daddy Laveau."

"Who's speaking?" My father asked teasing.

"The only person that should be calling you daddy hopefully." I answered with sarcasm.

"Then it must be my Scarlet Rose."

"It must be." I giggled.

Daddy and I caught up on our happenings since the last time we spoke. We kept it short and sweet as always. Daddy Laveau was never the one to hold long conversations on the phone. He said what was necessary and got off the phone. After we caught up he passed the phone to Momma Laveau.

"Scarlet darling. How's my baby girl?"
"She is just wonderful now."
"Missing your parents?"
"Always."
"Nothing is keeping you away but you."
"Momma don't start."
"Okay. I promise, but make plans to visit soon. I want to hold my baby."
"My word."

We talked for about a half an hour before saying I love you and handing the phone back to Daddy Laveau for the same. I couldn't have asked for better parents and my momma wouldn't have wanted a different child. Daddy Laveau however, would never admit that deep down inside he was terrified of what he assumed about me. My own daddy thought I was devil spun. He would never stop loving me but I could sense it from an early age that he feared and regretted something about me.

I recalled his calling me a little witch to my mother when I hurt a playmate for teasing me. That little rascal had called me a baby and pushed me to the concrete for not wanting to kiss him. I got a stick after him and beat him good. He had to have stitches by the time my daddy got me off of him. Momma Laveau defended my honor and told Daddy Laveau that if her baby was a witch then she was one too. My daddy responded by saying, "Maybe so but it would be the difference between you being a white witch and

Scarlet being a black one." They argued something awful beneath
their breath before my daddy apologized and my momma loved on
him afterwards.

I took a walk late in the evening. I needed to be one with
the universe to center my thoughts. Night and day I was consumed
with thoughts of murder. Even when I did not want to think about
murder, it came calling to me. I always got some type of rise from
reading about it or seeing it on television. I thought about how to
pull it off without getting caught and most of all, who would I
slaughter and why? Did I need a reason even? Maybe I could kill a
homeless person or someone that was ill. It would surely put them
out of their misery. A stranger just seemed too easy and had no
purpose though. I wouldn't know anything about them and so I
would still feel that void that I needed to fill so desperately. If I did
not slay someone really soon I was going to cause my own demise
by pondering over it in such a way. I did not even understand the
urgency that burned from within me to harm another. But it was
there just as sure as my name was Scarlet Rose Laveau. I guess
some things we are just born with and there is no justifiable reason
for it at all.

My neighborhood was an artsy venture, something that I
was very proud of. Some called it the Black Pearl. I do not know
why but it certainly felt like a jewel to me. I loved strolling the
block and taking in the scenery and the people that stared after
with fear, awe and envy. They filled me with a presence of power
as they whispered and turned to look away when I met their hungry
and accusing glances. Such cowards they were in public. Many had
paid me a visit to heal or cure one thing or another.

The neighborhood was also full of fucking hypocrites. I wanted to call out to old lady Margret's gossiping ass and ask if her young lover had ever returned her jewelry that he had stolen from her. I bet it would blow her neighbors away to know that she was sexing that bag boy down at the local mom and pop shop on the corner. And even more so that she had come to the so called "voodoo bitch" for help. Her dear friends would surely ostracize her for such behavior. Not to mention that each of those want-to-be Christians had also visited me in secret. I laughed aloud and must have seemed even crazier to them for doing so as I continued to walk the neighborhood.

Mike Mike was on the block tearing it up with his saxophone. He was so deep in concentration that he did not even notice me standing there. I dropped a few dollars on him for blessing us with such splendor. I would bet you that he had been in that same spot daily since I was old enough to roam the hood alone and even before. If he was not playing that sax he was sitting on his bucket looking toward heaven. He gawked at the sky as if he was waiting for a hand to reach down and snatch him up.

Mike Mike had to be around sixty now. He still looked young in his effort but he played tunes with an old man's soul. He was a poor man by trade but rich in spirit. No one would dare try and run him away from that curb. He was the neighborhood musician and we loved him so. If they could not give him money they brought him food or something to show their appreciation. The dude was odd but talented and magnificent. He had white hair that hung down his back in a single braid with a long mustache that was also braided. Mike Mike had red clay colored skin that shone and wrinkled from too much sun. He finally took notice of me and smiled.

"Scarlet Red."

"Mike Mike."

That is the most we ever said really. I would hang around for a few minutes as he played just for me and then I left.

As I continued strolling through our pie shaped vicinity, I ran into one of my favorite little people. Lilia was walking her beloved golden retriever Dexter. She was a gorgeous child. She made my heart skip all over the place with glee at her sight. Lilia was so very small for her eight years with long pigtails and skinny legs. She had Gerber baby eyes and a smile that would melt any stoned heart that came in contact with it.

Lilia marched up and down our street as if she owned it. Sometimes she would be crying her eyes out trying to get back home or inside a house that no longer belonged to her. I stopped to greet her with a hug and to pat the puppy. You should have seen the neighbors damn near breaking their necks to stare at me. They whispered something about me talking to myself. They could say what they wanted and claim not to believe in lost spirits. But they knew that Lilia still walked that block. Her soul was lost and unwilling to say goodbye to a life that was snatched away from her all too soon by a drunk driver. She would forever be with us or at least until someone in her family was brave enough to offer her peace.

I felt renewed after my afternoon stroll and returned home to prepare for my afternoon session. Koral was coming over to have a reading done since the last one we attempted never happened. She usually wanted a reading monthly but lately she had been coming by once a week. I had been helping Koral with her past, present and future for many years. What she was looking for would never happen. She lived in a fantasy world of wants and her needs were no different. I would do my best to try and convince her to follow another path other than the destructive one that she dreamed of. Sometimes I had to make up things to soothe her. She wanted to know more about her birth mother. Most of all she needed to know that she had been loved and that her mom wanted and tried to be with her. The truth about her mom was a selfish one, one that I could never reveal to my dearest friend. It would break her heart to know that Precious Baptiste only cared about her damn self.

Koral sat across from me teary eyed and shiny. The small round table was the only thing that bridged us apart. I ran my naked foot up and down her uncovered legs beneath the table as I continued her reading. She always got so emotional during my readings of her. It almost made me want to lie about it all to spare her some tears. Why couldn't I just tell her what she wanted to hear about both her mother and Nana.

"Scarlet, I worry over Nana still trying to do so much. Her back is beginning to bend and she is already looking a lot older than what she is."

"Yes, I have noticed."

"You know Nana as well as I do, she won't listen none. I beg her to just rest. Am I being too controlling or do I have the right to be worried?"

"If I told you not to…would you?"

"No." she said shaking her head.

She knew as well as I did that it would be pointless to ask her not to worry over a woman that was surely dying in her face. When you work hard you die hard. Koral's Nana had been dying since the day she was forced to find a way to survive. Her husband had up and died leaving her with a baby girl and no formal education. She had to use what natural skills she had to endure. Nana was already growing most of her food right in her own backyard. She was also baking goodies for the neighbors and always giving away her handmade jewelry as gifts. She used those daily things to turn a living after becoming a widow. Nana was now known as the veggie lady, the goody lady and the bead lady. She was quite a hit in New Orleans.

"Look Koral, I'm going to give it to you straight. Start looking for a life of your own. You won't be able to live off of Nana forever you know."

Koral sucked her teeth and looked at me as if I had lost my mind for saying that.

"Live off of Nana? I know I don't have a job Scarlet. But God as my witness, I pull my weight."

"I see." I said rolling my eyes at her impatient ear.

"If Nana would allow me to charge more for her items and rightfully so, we could make so much more money." She continued.

I gawked at Koral's absurdity. Sometimes it was so hard getting through to her. I lounged in my chair shaking my head while allowing my feet to greet her inner thigh.

"Don't be foolish woman. I know damn well that you are not using Nana in that way. I am saying that you use her as an excuse to avoid living your own life. "

"Hmph."

"Don't you want anything for yourself Koral? What about your dreams?"

The tears started to flow one behind the other as she gave me the same sorry ass excuse as she always had. Koral said that someone had to look after Nana and that she was all there was. I just knew that Nana would find a way to be okay. Because she knew like I did that if Koral did not find her own way soon, she would be left helpless and needy. As gorgeous as Koral was, there was nothing she could do without Nana but maybe sell her pussy to survive.

The thought of her vagina sent my mind racing down below my belly button and I felt my clit rise to attention. I massaged Koral with my toes and watched the frustration drain from her face into want. We would worry about what to do about her and Nana later. It was time to suppress my appetite. I went to Koral and kneeled down beside her placing my chin on her thigh. She felt so smooth and so warm and inviting. Was I wrong to stare up in her teary diamond shaped eyes and reveal my thoughts during a time like that?

"I will help you figure it all out." I promised as I imagined her big mouth over my lower lips.

Koral caressed my face with her gentle but determined hands.
"I love you Scarlet." She confessed with too much love.
"I love you too." I replied with just enough love to get me by.
I got up and went to sit on my Momma Laveau's couch. It was mine now, but I like the idea that it once belonged to her. It was long, sofa shaped, much like a sled and made of the same mahogany wood as the record player. The seating section was finished with canary yellow crushed velvet and there were two

bolster pillows at each end. I found myself fantasizing about my parents walking in and catching Koral lost between my thighs. It reminded me of the many times we almost got caught when we were still teens making out in any private space we could find. I pulled away from my fantasy to find Koral's eyes ablaze and her hand fondling the uncovered place I wished to be. It was time for me to take control of the situation. I claimed her eyes once again with mine and made my commands.

"I am your God and you are my Goddess and anything I ask of you should be given freely. Do you follow me Koral?"

"Yes."

"Yes what?"

"Yes my God. Whatever I have to offer is yours." Koral obeyed while spreading her lips to offer her sodden bud to me.

"I don't want that! Close your legs and crawl to me. I have needs far greater than yours."

"What would you like for me to do?" Koral asked.

"Close your fucking mouth."

I laughed while leaning back on the sofa and spreading my legs to capacity. Koral closed her mouth like a good girl.

"I meant… close your mouth over my pussy and make my heart race until it burst into flames. Can you handle that my Goddess?" I continued.

"May I answer my God?"

"Your reply should be your tongue approaching my anxious clit."

I laid my head back and closed my eyes to receive Koral. Her tongue felt like heaven swelled up inside of me. I heard angels singing or maybe it was me crying out.

"Deeper my love, deeper."

She got lost in my valley and had no intentions of finding her way out.

"What does it taste like my Goddess?" I moaned while breathing erratically.

Koral kept right on squeezing the life out of my clit.

"Take your face out of my pussy for a second and answer your God!" I demanded.

"May I speak?" Koral pleaded with misted lips.

"Yes. Come kiss me and tell."

Koral straddled me on the sofa while trying to suck my face off. I pulled away after a moment and offered her a tongue dance.

"My God, your pussy tastes like the sweetest nectar from the rarest flower. And I patiently wait for your consent to absorb more." Koral replied between tongue lashings.

I licked around Koral's lips to savor my own juices. "You may return to drink from my honey well until it runs dry. But only if you have a unique way to do so?" I asked.

Koral moved to position her face back between my gapped thighs. I pushed them closed, not allowing her access.

"That was a question, and you should share your plans before delighting yourself." I ordered.

"I would like to absorb your honey lick by lick my God."

"NO!" I screamed. I am not satisfied with your lame ass answer. Must I beat you to get what I want?"

I rose leaving her kneeling before me. And before I knew it a rage consumed me and my hand elevated the temperature in Koral's right cheek. Her head twisted slightly before she turned back to meet my fuming gaze. She was infatuated and more than ready to continue.

"You are pissing me the fuck off Koral!" I announced while plopping back down onto the sofa.

Koral stayed obedient with her head now bowed and apologetic. "I am very sorry my God."

"Get up here and let me show you how it's done you amateur bitch." I said while helping her settle her even plumper lips over mine. I opened wide to receive all that Koral had to offer. The night was young and I had plans to feed well.

Koral and I lay on the sofa conversing after our rendezvous was over. We caught up on time missed and other things floating around in our minds like going on vacation together one day. We always wanted to get out of the country. If it was not for Nana we probably would have been several places together by then. I pretended to listen to Koral continue fantasizing over us living on some deserted and exotic island. I would have gone fucking nuts being stranded in a foreign place with one woman to my name. Koral was as loony and naive as they came. I don't know what made her think that we could be together like that ever. But who would I be to crush her dreams? After all she was my best friend ever and the only living soul I could speak about my cravings for murder to and not be judged. What I wanted for Koral after all was said and done was a good husband and many babies to keep her happy. I would always be there for her to love on when she needed something extra but I wasn't the settling kind. I pulled myself from Koral's embrace as she continued to chatter about nothing.

"Where are you going?" Koral asked with her long and innocent face tilted to one side.

"I have something that I want to show you." I said with way too much excitement.

Koral sat up looking curious as ever as I disappeared into the back of the house. I returned soon enough standing in the archway of the living room still nude but now with a nineteen sixty-two Colt Python. It was a bright nickel colored three-fifty-seven Magnum caliber revolver. I pointed it straight at Koral. I could hear her heart reach its peak in that moment. It damn near pounded out of her chest.

"What are you doing with that Scarlet Rose Laveau?"

I walked toward her with the gun still aimed in her direction. I could feel her nerves giving way to the trust we had built up throughout the years. The fear that she had for me then was far greater than any other time.

"Put that thing away Scarlet." Koral instructed in a weakened voice.

I put the gun to her forehead and placed my finger on the trigger as I stared in her dilating eyeballs. They were troubled, lonely and confused. In that instant Koral actually thought I would shoot her. I smiled at her stupidity before removing the revolver and bursting into uncontrollable laughter.

"How could you ever assume that I would hurt you?" I teased.

Koral sat shaking and crying.

"Come on Koral, I would never harm you, I love you."

"I know that, you are just so foolish sometimes and accidents can happen. I have always been afraid of guns. How did you get that?" She asked.

"It belonged to Daddy Laveau. He left it for protection is all. He said I may need it one day with a profession and reputation like mine." I said while putting the firearm down to comfort my friend.

I pushed the tears from Koral's eyes and took her into my arms. Her skin was always extra warm and damp against my cold body.

"Koral?"

"Yes Scarlet?"

"You believed me when I said I could never hurt you, Right?"

"Yes Scarlet." She lied.

"Good, because your loyalty and faith means everything to me."

Koral looked up at me and smiled. She wanted to believe me but her intuition would not let her forget how I lusted after her terror. And even if she did not believe me, her love for me was enough to keep her friendship entrusted forever.

After Koral left that night, I lay in bed thinking about murder as usual and my target. All of a sudden several people came to mind. It was as if a messenger was standing before me with an outline on how to proceed with not only pulling off the perfect murder but also the perfect people to butcher. There were no strangers on the hit list; all of the people were familiar. The only problem I had now was choosing which one. They were all so very tempting.

Chapter Eight
Koral

The work day had been a long one. I was almost out of everything but a few green tomatoes and several pieces of bead jewelry. It was close to sundown and I wanted to pack up and head home before the streetlights caught up with me.

"Fixin to go Koral?"

I turned around to face Carmelite's half charred face. She had been a victim of spousal abuse for years. You could hear her then husband Henri beating her from miles away at times. We were always told to mind our place and our business. So nobody ever tried to help her. I was still small when Carmelite's husband set the house on fire while she and her baby girl slept. Henri had left and went to have a drink while his family was burning to death. The fire department barely got Carmelite out alive. When they pulled her out she was walking up the stairs on fire trying to get to her baby girl Lisette. Lisette had died from smoke inhalation. Carmelite lost her mind on the count of it and had to be institutionalized for a long time. She was never the same when the county finally let her out of the hospital.

"Hey there Carmelite. I'm out of everything but these here green tomatoes. Want to take them off my hand?"
"How many you got there. I only need one." She said counting out her change to hand to me.

I knew it would offend Carmelite not to take her money and so I held out my hand to receive it.

I handed over the bag of tomatoes after placing the change in my pocket.

Carmelite looked into the bag and then back at me. "I said one Koral!"

Last thing I needed was Carmelite losing it on me. I was tired and ready to get home and into a hot bath.

"I know Carmelite. But this here basket is really heavy and you would be doing me a favor by taking them all. Pretty please?" I lied with the best smile I could pull up.

"Okay Koral. You sure is pretty and awfully nice. You remind me of my Lisette. She had a spirit much like yours." Carmelite reminisced with her depressing face.

"Thank you Carmelite. I'll see you next time. I need to get home to Nana."

"Tell her hello. And tell Scarlet that I will be back when I get my check next month?"

"I will Carmelite. Goodnight." I said while moving in the direction of my home.

Carmelite would spend her last dime trying to visit Scarlet and get her to channel Lisette's spirit. Nana thought that Scarlet was wrong for taking Carmelite's money. She said that Scarlet would have done it from the kindness of her heart had she owned one. I told Nana not everyone wanted to give their gifts away for free and that Scarlet had to make a living like everyone else. Carmelite would never take nothing for free anyhow. Though, it was no use in defending Scarlet to Nana because she hated her. She would hear nothing good along with the mention of Scarlet's name. It was a hopeless situation that I prayed on daily.

Once I reached the steps of my home I had to pause short
of climbing the few steps to my door. My head started pounding
out of the blue and my chest tightened. I sat down on one of the
lower cemented steps and rubbed my forehead as if it would bring
me comfort. I took a deep breath praying that Nana would not walk
out and find me looking helpless. She had enough to worry over as
it was and I didn't want to add to it. I looked over at one of the tiny
flower beds on one side of the steps. The wind blew but the
flowers stood still. They wanted me to notice them but my mind
quickly dismissed the message. I stood to gather myself thinking
that a nice hot soak would relieve the pressure that my body felt.

As soon as I opened the door I was greeted with loud
church music coming from Nana's radio and the smell of fish and
yams. The aroma hit me smack in the face. They were two of my
favorite dishes and I was starved. I decided to hurry with my bath
so that I could stuff my face while telling myself that maybe I had
hunger aches.

"Nana how was your day?" I yelled out but didn't wait for
an answer.

She would talk from that point anyway. At times Nana
would still be talking after I finished bathing as if I had been sitting
right there in front of her listening.

I quickly removed my clothes while filling the tub with
steaming hot water. The water was loud and the plumbing was
shaky. We had one of the old deep claw foot tubs. It leaked
sometimes and needed to be replaced but served its purpose. I
made sure to put a towel down before stepping into the tub to catch
any water that decided to seep out.

Thoughts of Scarlet filled my mind swiftly. We had
enjoyed many baths together over the years. I loved sharing those
moments with her. Sometimes I wondered if my obsession with
her was indecent. My hands wanted to be tangled up in her ruby

locked hair while massaging her head the way she like it. Scarlet's locs were so long that they intimidated me with the strength that they embodied. It was hard remembering when she had a head full of soft strawberry curls. It must have been our early teen years that Scarlet decided to loc her hair. She was attractive with or without the locs. But they gave her a Goddess appeal. I would love that woman bald if that is what she decided.

Her face was enough to keep me satisfied for life. She had this natural sex appeal about her. Scarlet's eyes were oceans of wonder, and her lips were shaped like a heart with a beauty mark right beneath the lower lip. I wanted to suck it off her face. Thoughts of her turned my bath into a romantic adventure down Scarlet lane. My bath lasted longer than I had planned. I wrapped up my day dreams of Scarlet to finish washing. *Give it a break will you?*

"Fish and yams, fish and yams." I sang out loud as I stopped by Nana's room to see what I did to deserve my favorite meal. Her radio was loud as ever. Nana's hearing must have been going, because it seemed as if she played that radio and television louder as the days passed. Nana was not in her room as I had assumed. I would have to get her another radio for the kitchen so that she would not have to turn it up so loud to hear it from another room. Her birthday was coming up soon and it would be a great gift. I hurried to the kitchen to greet Nana and to grab my plate that would be waiting in the oven to keep warm.

Nana was not in the kitchen either. There were only two other places she could be. Either she was in her garden or sitting on Mrs. Monroe's back porch visiting with her. They were about the same age and both widowed. Nana and Mrs. Monroe kept an eye on the other.

I grabbed my plate from the oven almost burning my hand on the count of forgetting to use the oven mitten.

"Ouch!" I cried out.

But that did not stop me from eating at all. I filled my mouth with a big chunk of sweet potato while sitting my plate down. I went to the backdoor to look for Nana. It was slightly dark out and getting darker by the minute. I pulled the long thin and dirty white string to turn the porch light on. *Nana why would you not have the porch light on by now. Guess she is down at Mrs. Monroe's.*

I stepped down the steps looking around for my old lady. She would need to be much more considerate of visiting folks at night. A note would have been plenty. *I will just go down to Mrs. Monroe's and walk Nana back when she is ready to leave.* I didn't like the idea of her being alone at the house let alone walking alone from somebody else's.

Just as I stepped off the last step I noticed Nana's pink and green floral house dress. I walked closer to get a better look hoping that it had fell from the clothing line. It was Nana lumped over in the dirt with an expression of defeat. I stood as still as the flowers that had greeted me in the front yard and as still as the vegetables that were surrounding my Nana beneath a rising moon.

"Nana?" I barely spoke above a whisper. "Nana now just you get up from there!" I shouted out this time.

I dropped to my knees hard on the dirt not caring about the pain. I felt something leave me in that moment, but realized that there was no time to be selfish. This was not about me. I needed to help my Nana and make sure she wasn't hurt. I needed to help her in the house to her bed. *I should have been here with you. I should not have been leaving you alone.* I crawled to her like when I was an infant in search of her care. She was in need of mine now. *Why have I not been caring for you? I will do it every day from now on.*

I reached for Nana and shook her real good I shook her so good that her body gave way and she fell over completely. Her expression was an eerie one that left me as breathless as she seemed to be.

"Nana oh Nana. I am so sorry."

I covered my mouth and sobbed. My Nana was gone. I double checked for a beat in her throat because maybe I was wrong. I checked again in her heart and in her wrist but there was nothing but silence in her worn body.

"Why did you leave me Nana, you know how much I need you here with me." I said to nothing but a shell of a woman.

I lay with Nana's shell and crawled up in her arms the best I could and snuggled under her wrinkled neck to smell her honeydew scented body one last time. I cried for her life taken and what my life was going to be without her. I rocked with Nana's corpse for a while. I knew once the coroner came and took her from me that she would be gone forever.

"Take it back God, I need my Nana. You know how much I need my Nana and you done gone and snatch her from me."

Did God not understand that I too was entitled to some type of family? Just what was his purpose in all of this? I had been a good girl for my Nana. No trouble had I caused her or my momma and yet they both were taken from me.

"You already done took my grandpa and my momma. What else you gone take from me? I ain't got nothing else. Take it back God, give my Nana back." I sobbed.

I had called Scarlet over to the house after finding the strength to get up from under Nana's body. Scarlet caught a cab right over and was by my side supporting me as she always had.

"I didn't know who else to call." I said to Scarlet.

"Oh Koral, I am so sorry, come to me." Scarlet said embracing my breaking spirit.

Being in Scarlet's arms made me weaker and I cried heavily. I could not quite believe that my Nana was gone. I had tried to bring her into the house with no success.

"Let us get Nana in the house Koral. Are you going to be able to help me?"

"Yes." I replied trying to find the courage to do so. I did not want to leave Nana out there any longer.

Scarlet headed to the backyard ahead of me. I was so grateful that she was there and that I was no longer alone. We picked Nana up and carried her into the house and placed her onto the sofa in the front room. Scarlet and I both stood staring down at Nana. I turned my back to her to keep from looking into her locked and lost looking eyes.

Scarlet took her finger and closed Nana's eyes. "I closed them. You can turn back around now."

Scarlet always knew what to do without me saying a word.

I turned back around to face my Nana again. Nana looked as if she was just sleeping now. I sat down on the floor beside her body and caressed her face. *What am I going to do?*

"You are going to come stay with me. We will figure everything else out from there." Scarlet said reading my mind again.

"I do not want to leave Nana, Scarlet."

"She will not be here baby."

With those words I broke down. My body fell limp as I soaked the floor with my tears. "Nanaaaaaaa." I wept.

Scarlet called for the coroner. She was doing the things that I should have been doing but could not gather myself to do.

I could hear her giving details and directions to my home. They were coming to take my Nana away from me. It all seemed like a really bad nightmare that I prayed to wake up from.

"Scarlet, what am I going to do without my Nana? For twenty-five years it has been me and Nana."

"Yes, I know baby. You are going to live the life she would have wanted for you. I need you to help me wash Nana up and get her ready for the coroner. You know she would just die all over again if she knew we sent her off in this house dress."

That made me laugh a little. What Scarlet said had been true about Nana. Had she known that she was going to die today, Nana would have bathed and put on her Sunday's best.

"Scarlet?"

"Yes Koral?"

"Did Nana have a heart attack or a stroke or something?"

"It was natural causes Koral, Nana did not feel a thing she just fell over done. Done with living. She is at peace now and wants you to be okay."

Scarlet and I talked about good times with Nana as we gave her a sponge bath and dressed her. Her hair was the last thing that needed to be done and I wanted to be the one to brush it. I loved my Nana's silky and wavy long silver hair. She had been a looker once. Petite and beautiful. I just wished that life would have been a little easier for her. If only we could turn time around and make the best of it. I had stuff that I wanted to tell my Nana. I needed to love on her one last time and thank her for being my momma all these years. It was the saddest day of my life and my heart was hurting something awful.

Part 2

Chapter Nine
Scarlet

Koral had lost her Nana. Nana was the only mother she had ever known. A woman that was more than just a grandmother to her, she was also Koral's caregiver in many ways. She provided for her both emotionally and monetarily. I had warned Koral many of times to make life work for her without the crutches. I told her that Nana was not promised to her forever. But she would not hear of her old lady dying. Now I would have to care of Koral until she was able to care for herself. She was special to me and I would never see her on the streets without the work skills she needed. Koral did not have a green thumb to grow vegetables on her own and she could not cook all that well either. She lacked the skills needed to do the art work for the beaded jewelry. Koral had none of Nana's natural talent and though she had tried to learn, she had failed miserably. Nana had been the backbone of it all. Koral had simply pushed the products when Nana was too weak to do so.

Nana's small insurance policy barely covered the cost of her funeral. After Koral paid off the monthly bills at their house there was nothing left except two-hundred dollars. Nana had tucked it away in the kitchen cabinet above the refrigerator. We found that money while cleaning out the house. The landlord wanted Koral out. He was well aware that she would not be able to afford the rent. After Nana's funeral we packed up the house and moved Koral to my home.

I felt deeply for my friend and the loss of Nana. Nana had once meant a lot to me as well. She would still pretend that she cared whenever I was around but I knew that old lady hated me for things that I could not help. Koral would always make excuses if I brought the subject up. Truth be told, and not that I would ever say it to Koral, but she was better off now. She had been freed.

Although Nana had cared for her, Koral did not have a life on the count of feeling that she owed Nana her life. They had both been trying to make up life for the other. There is no making up life. We can only move on with what we know and have.

The night that we placed Nana's body on the sofa, I heard her breathe a little. That look in her eyes let me know that something more than natural causes had occurred. I closed her eyes to keep from seeing the little bit of life left in her. I asked Koral to fetch some water and clean clothes to freshen Nana up. I needed Koral out of the room because I did not want Koral to have to lose her Nana twice. Even if Nana did live it would not have been for long and Koral would have to lose even more than she had. There was no fight left in Nana and so it was an easy take. I picked up one of the squared pillows with tassels all around it and gently helped Nana to the other side where she belonged. Nana would get to be with her beloved husband and daughter again and Koral could get on with learning how to live.

I thought I would feel some type of power for helping Nana finish dying but I felt cheated. She was already half dead and also it was a call of mercy that I had committed, not murder. It benefitted Nana more than it did me and I was far from satisfied.

It was still really early in the morning as I lay in bed obsessing over my murder plot and Nana's death. Koral was still fast asleep in my parents room. It had only been several months since Nana's passing. Koral had found work at a restaurant down in the French Quarters waiting tables. It was not that much but it was a start and better than nothing.

My thoughts were all over the place from murder to Koral when I heard what sounded like a hammer at my front door. I jumped from the bed and stormed through the house to see who had the nerve to knock so harshly at such an hour. The sun had barely peeked through the sky and some idiot was about to knock my door down.

"Who is it?" I demanded in a not so pleasant voice.

"Police. Open up Ms. Laveau." Some feminine but deep voice commanded.

She knew me but I didn't know her. But then again mostly everyone knew Scarlet Laveau. I opened up the door to greet the officer and her partner while peering at her badge and purposely ignoring the other officer.

"Brazil Tio. How may I help you?" I asked as visions of me smothering Nana gathered in my head.

"Ms. Laveau we were called to the scene of an apparent suicide early this morning and your name came up as a possible reason as to why the suicide took place. We just want to ask you some questions if you don't mind," Officer Tio said while the other officer stood as quiet as a toy soldier.

"Suicide? Why on earth would my name come up? Who is the victim?" I asked looking Officer Tio dead in her seductive and troubled eyes.

She was very handsome for a woman. Someone had been quite generous with her. Her dark hair was pulled back in a neat bun and her uniform was just as precise. Brazil Tio's eyes smiled at the corners. I stared trying to figure out her nationality. There was a hint of Native-American with a good portion of African-American and maybe half German mixed up in her.

"Jessie French was the victim." Officer Tio answered with a bit of anxiety.

"I do not know of him." I lied in a way. I had met him that one time but I didn't know him.

"Sure you do. He came to you earlier this year for a reading."

"Many people come to me for a reading Officer Tio." I said holding my position with a straight face.

"But not with the same names I am sure. Do you keep a schedule of your customers?"

"I do. But what is it to you?"

"Well Ms. Laveau, Jessie went missing shortly after he visited you."

"Are you implying anything here?

Officer Brazil shifted her weight back and forth as if her tight and shiny black shoes were punishing her feet.

"He left his family a note stating that he was dying and they would be better off without him. He also mentioned that you told him that he only had a year to live." Officer Brazil said.

"I told him no such thing. And if I had, it would have been the truth."

"So you remember him?"

"I am remembering, go on."

"They have been searching for him since, only to be called down to the coroner's office last night to identify his body… well what was left of it. Some boater discovered it down by the bayou."

There was a blank look on my face. I couldn't pretend to care that this stranger was dead. The world was better off with him not spreading that virus he had.

"Look Officer Tio, folks pay for services and I render them. I am not responsible for what they do. But the things that Jessie wrote in that letter were not true. I never told him that he was dying and what I did tell him is in the strictest of confidence. Now if you will leave so that I may return to my slumber." I said while stepping back and turning to close the door.

Officer Tio stepped closer to me.

"Ms. Laveau?"

"Yes?" I said turning back to look at her in a very seductive way."

"This is not over."

I smiled at the lovely thing before me. "How right you are." I replied while shutting my door.

Koral was still fast asleep and snoring lightly. That woman could sleep through a bulldozer tearing the house down. But if a feather fell I would awake instantly. I returned to my bed to try and catch a few more hours before I had to be up for a channeling with Ms. Carmelite. She was one of my favorite people. Folks thought she was nuts but she was just hurting like most of the world. I finally fell back asleep just to dream about Brazil Tio. What kind of name was that for a girl child? Maybe her father had wanted a boy. She could definitely be an androgynous.

It was early evening time. Carmelite loved to travel with the arrival of the moon. She felt that it hid her unsightliness. Never had I viewed the mark of cruelty that her husband Henri left her with as unpleasant. It was only a reminder of what limitations could do to the soul of a woman. If I could give Carmelite my face I would without hesitation. Because I knew that I was bold enough to wear my flaws in the sun. I refused to allow mere humans to make me take cover when they were all blemished in different but equal ways. I tried to convey this to Carmelite but her spirit was broken in such a way that her missing pieces were impossible to mend. With what I had to gift, I did what I could to bring Carmelite her needs.

Carmelite joined me eager to get started. She never wanted to waste time before the readings.

"Carmelite, may I come into your vibration?" I requested
"Yes Scarlet, you may enter."

The room was dark, cool and alluring. There was a single candle burning bright in the middle of the round and personalized table. Carmelite sat across from me anxious and as relaxed as possible. I saw her in three dimensions, as a mother, a child and the warrior she had been centuries ago. I left my physical body to travel through her world and find what she sought. I moved with ease, caution and determination. There was a path of flames that encircled an apple tree and beneath that tree was a girl child by the name of Lisette. She was pleasantly plump and highly favored in the face. I approached the flames and awaited an invitation. Lisette held out her approving hand and batted her lengthy eyelashes. She was a charmer and at the age she would have been in the physical world. This was a gem to find in channeling because most spirits stayed their same age at death for eternity in the afterlife. Lisette was growing every day too. It was obvious that her mission was one that only her adult person could execute. Her plans for revenge on her father Henri alarmed and excited me at the same time. Lisette had fire for eyes and a razor sharp tongue. This child was hell camouflaged as heaven. She was so much like Henri but had also possessed the tenderness for Carmelite. I spoke from my spirit through my physical body that sat dazed in a wooden chair ahead of Carmelite.

"I have found Lisette. What is it that you seek today?"

"Tell her I love her and miss her every minute. Tell her that I wish I could do that day all over again. Ask her if there is anything that she needs?" Carmelite said in teary pain.

"Lisette's only desire is for you to be happy again. She is brave and without necessity. She sends her love and wants to hold you if that is okay?"

Carmelite wiped the tears away from her eyes and smiled with unease. "Please. Tell her I am waiting."

Lisette took hold of my hand and we walked through the flames into the living world of my living room, where Carmelite sat restless. I glanced over at my body as I always did when I walked in the spirit. It was like glancing into a mirror. I noted that I had aged slightly and was looking more like a woman. It appeased me. Lisette let go of my hand to approach Carmelite. She placed her ample arms around her mother and laid her head on Carmelite's shoulders.

"Lisette is holding you now Carmelite."

"I miss you so much Lisette. I pray to join you soon baby. Your momma loves you. Tell me about her again Scarlet. Please tell me about my baby." The tears were pouring as Carmelite's body rocked.

"She is twelve now, as you know, with a plentiful frame and with the face of an angel. Her brunette curls are about to her waistline now. She has your liking before the fire. Lisette is a warrior like you once were Carmelite."

Lisette moved forward to view her mother's face. Her small chubby hands slid down the length of Carmelites scarred face. I felt sorrow and then anger from Lisette and with that her spirit started to fade.

"Lisette is leaving us Carmelite. Any last words?"

"Why so soon? Is she still angry with Henri?

"Yes. She said that she is always watching over you and to try and find a new reason to live for. She loves you with all that she has."

"Tell her she has to forgive in order to find a resting place."

"I have told her on my many visits. She is determined to do it her way Carmelite but I will try on our next session because Lisette has returned to her world."

I watched Lisette's dimmed spirit burst into a cloud of flames that sent my spirit racing back into my body. I woke with a loud heart and a concerned Carmelite.

"Don't worry Carmelite. I will take good care of Lisette. We are good friends now. She trusts me." I smiled.

"Good. I thank you Ms. Scarlet. Lawd knows what I'd do without your kind. I'm fixin to go now." Carmelite said rising from her seat.

I walked Carmelite out with a hug and more reassurance. It saddened me to see her journey life alone. Henri did not deserve to breathe. I was more than grateful that Lisette would see to his demise.

The night was still young and I had a ceremony to attend. It was a dance used to honor the gods. Before attending my event, I had to drop off some of my homemade herbs to Lady Soule just up the road. She had bad knees on the count of an automobile accident. Lady Soule had tried many different prescribed medications by her doctor before turning to me. Momma Laveau had provided healing herbs to the locals for years and I had learned everything I knew from her. I was so much more than a palm reader. I could do many things concerning the body, mind and spirit. Over the years both Momma Laveau and I had helped our neighbors overcome ailments that professional physicians could not cure with their experimental drugs.

Lady Soule came to my door desperately searching freedom from pain one late night some years ago. She had been a loyal customer of mine now for nearly six years. I made a special healing balm that kept Lady Soule a loyal customer.

I checked over my all white garment in the mirror before me. It made me feel pure to be dressed in such a way. I tucked my brightly colored apron and headscarf into my bag. We used the ceremonial clothing to pay homage to those that have been and also for which we have come from.

That night we performed a dance of supplication. I was in love with the music and the rave. I waited impatiently for the sound of the drum to initiate the ceremonial dance. At times we would dance so hard that our arms and shoulders would move so violently. But in the true spirit form of an offering you felt no pain and so it was all very enjoyable. It was a divine thing to experience. I was able to release and receive what was needed.

Koral had begged me something awful to allow her to join in on the ceremonies. But she was not ready. Although Koral never really went to church like that, she was very religious in her thinking because of Nana. Koral would go from being awed by the stories that I shared with her of the ceremonies to being adverse about them. She always wanted to tell me about Nana saying that we could not serve two masters. I told her that it was nonsense to believe in limitations.

What Koral thought or did not think about my beliefs did not keep me from sharing everything with her. I just decided against taking her to any of the ceremonies until she was for certain that she was ready to enter that world. It was a lot different from the homemade Christian teachings of her Nana and she would need to be ready. To hear about the ceremonies was one thing but to experience them would be life changing. She would be ready on the day that her spirit was open to understand things beyond those hypocritical teachings of Nana.

I knew in my heart that Koral was not ready for much of anything but some good old love and friendship. She was still grieving the death of her world and trying desperately to fit into a new one that she knew nothing about, a world where real responsibility existed.

I placed my beads around my slender neck. It was a necklace of honor. It honored the Four Winds Goddess. She is a friend of our ancestors and those who have passed on from the physical world. She is stronger than any man and more beautiful than any woman dead or alive. She reflected my soul and so I wore the beads to honor us both. I left my home skipping and singing.

"I'm off to see the Wizard the wonderful Wizard of us all." I continued singing. I was eager to drop off the herbs to Lady Soule so that I could connect with the divinity and my spirit world.

Chapter Ten
Koral

The loss of my Nana was the hardest ordeal that I had ever faced. Some days it was hard to pull myself out of bed and other days I wished that I had died right with her. It was where I belonged, with my grandpa, Nana and mother. We could be a family again like Nana had promised me that we would be someday. *God I miss my Nana. I can still hear her so very clearly.*

I would have stayed in bed forever if I knew how to be selfish. But there was no way that I could leave Scarlet to fend for us both. It was more than enough that she had taken me in. I knew that I had to pull my weight and help out with the bills in order not to feel guilty. Scarlet would never ask me for anything. She said that the bills did not change with me being there and that it was her business to take care of her home. Even with Scarlet feeling like that, I still needed money for my own personal needs.

Nana had a name in the Crescent City and on the strength of that I was able to find a job down in The French Quarters. The job only paid minimum wage but it was plenty money to live on and save up with Scarlet refusing to take a dime. Scarlet said that I could stay in her home forever if I wanted as long as I respected her space. I took that as a need to work hard and save up enough to get my own space when and if needed. I didn't want to take so much and not give anything back and so I set some of my pay aside for Scarlet without her knowledge. When and if she ever found herself in need of the extra money, it would be there waiting.

I waited tables at a seafood restaurant that sold all of the famous New Orleans cuisines like gumbo and fried seafood. The joint had been around for damn near one hundred years. Although their food was wonderful, it was not better than my Nana's. She should have opened a restaurant and shared her gift with the world and not just a few with that damn veggie stand. Nana just wasted away slaving herself for pennies a day. I knew that Nana did not want me feeling that way about her because she was proud of the ability to take care of herself, but it just was not enough. I just kept wishing that she could have had more than hard days but there was nothing I could do about it now. I guess I would be following in her footsteps if I did not figure out how to better my life soon.

Paul came over to Scarlet's place to have a talk with me. He had been putting some heavy pressure on me to make a decision about our future since Nana died. He was always talking about us getting married but he seemed somewhat desperate since I had to move in with Scarlet. He kept saying things like, "I am your man and should be caring for you now." Part of my problem was people taking care of me and me never learning how to do it on my own. Well things were about to change and no man was going to leave me high and dry like my Grandpa Samuel had done to my Nana.

I sat on the porch waiting for Paul to arrive. Scarlet had been out late night and I did not want to disturb her with our talking. It was a nice day out with a slight chill in the air and still early enough for the sun light to last through what I would tolerate from Paul. I held my body tight and rocked a little to comfort myself from the hole in my heart while awaiting Paul's arrival.

I covered my mouth and stood up when I realized that it was Paul who had pulled up in a seemingly new shiny black Chevy Impala. *What in the world?!* Paul was actually driving a car and it was a really nice one. I could not hold in my smile when I heard the booty music spilling from the car speakers. I did not want to seem too anxious by running up to the car and so I held my body in place. I moved slightly over to make just enough room for Paul to sit beside me on the steps.

He stepped out that grand car looking just as new and vibrant as it.

"Hey there gal of mine."

"Pierre DePaul! I am nobody's gal. Now you call me by my proper name or you do not call on me at all. You hear me?" I said with a giggle.

Paul took a seat next to me and moved his hat from his head to his lap.

"Ms. Koral, I'm going to just say what I came here to say. I come here for you and I got something to sway you this time." He said while tugging at something in his pocket.

I looked on curious from him to the car. "Paul, where did you get that fancy car from and why are you dressed so fine on an ordinary day?"

"It is no ordinary day lady. And that there car is not only mine but yours as well Koral."

"What do you mean by mine?"

"I mean if you would have me. I don't have much left Koral. Just enough to get us where we are going in style and a lil more to last til I find some work."

I hesitated before speaking. "And where might *we*, be going?"

"New York, California, hell even Texas. I do not care woman. Just you pick and let us get out of here." Paul said with a straight face.

"Paul I…"

"Don't speak just yet. Not before you open my gift."

Paul handed me a small box wrapped in gold foil and trimmed in a red bow.

"It is much too early for Christmas." I said with fear in my voice.

"Stop talking woman and get that there thing open."

I ripped the paper from the box knowing what it would be. Paul took off his jacket and threw it to the ground below the steps and kneeled before me. The last thing I wanted to do was break his heart. I stared at the small but beautiful yellow gold and diamond ring. The tears started before I could wipe them away. Out of shame I jumped up and ran into the house.

"Damn girl!" Paul said with sincerity as he followed me in.

I forgot all about Scarlet resting as I lost what little control I had.

"Come on Koral, say yes. We belong together." Paul whined behind me.

"Paul, just sit and be quiet for a moment please."

Paul sat down on the couch and tapped his feet nervously. I could hear Scarlet in the shower and was thankful that I had not disturbed her sleep.

"This is sweet and I really wish I could but I can't." I said wiping the tears from my swelling eyes.

"What the fuck?!" Paul said standing to pace the floor.

"What reason do you have to stay here Koral?"

"My job and, and well...Scarlet." I replied.

"That shitty job? You can do better and hell... I can take care of you. Scarlet does not need you like I do. She will always be here and you can visit her anytime you want. I promise." He lied.

"I'm not leaving Paul." I said handing him back his ring.

"Koral baby girl, don't do this yet. Just wear it please. I won't rush you none. Put it on Koral, put it on now." He said refusing the ring and sitting back down on the sofa with glossy eyes.

I looked at Paul's pitiful self and placed the ring on my hand. I guess I could admire it while thinking of an easier way to let him down. He deserved at least that. I took a seat next to Paul on the sofa. He grabbed my hand and smiled at the ring for awhile.

The smell of fresh cherry blossoms filled the air. It was one of Scarlet's favorite body oil scents to wear.

"Why hello Pierre." Scarlet said.

She wore a crooked grin and a lot of loathing as she walked toward us.

"Good evening Scarlet." Paul matched her tone and sincerity.

Scarlet joined us on the sofa as if she had been invited. I knew she did it to torture Paul and usually it would have been funny but it wasn't the right time. The poor guy was going through enough with my rejection.

"What's that little sparkly thing on your hand Koral?"

I placed my hand on the ring and traced it. "Paul proposed."

"Oh really... hmm. Well, congratulations you two." Scarlet said and jumped to her feet.

"Thanks." I responded while waiting for Scarlet's next move.

"We should have a toast." Scarlet said.

I knew damn well that Scarlet was more than aware that I had turned Paul down. She was being specious. I could not help but laugh a little inside while boiling in the face. I jumped up to follow her into the kitchen. She was retrieving drinking glasses and Bourbon.

Scarlet turned to face me.

"What are you doing?" I asked.

"About to celebrate with you and Pierre."

"What for?"

"You know what for she said kissing my lips."

"Stop being a brute Scarlet Rose Laveau. I didn't say yes."

"Then why are you wearing that stupid ring." She teased.

Scarlet could be really wicked at times. This was a sensitive situation and I did not want to have her poking fun at Paul. He was nice enough and did not deserve Scarlet's phony celebration. Just because I had no plans to wed the man did not imply that I had to mistreat him as well.

"You better behave Scarlet."

"Or else what? You gonna whip me?"

"I just might."

"And I just might like it. Now stop being an ass and have a drink. No harm in a toast to whatever."

Scarlet returned to the living area with me in tow and Paul smiling as if Scarlet really believed we were engaged. He took the bottle from Scarlet's hand to open it and filled the empty glasses.

"May you two get everything you deserve and so much more." Scarlet said with a smirk.

Paul raised his glass to ours and stared straight at Scarlet. "Likewise."

Scarlet continued to pick fun at Paul while she drank down the Bourbon and stuffed her face with Beignets, a treat that we usually had with Café au Lait. They were her favorite, a treat that Nana used to make for us when we were girls. Scarlet's finger was covered in powdered sugar and instead of her wiping it on the cloth on her lap, she licked it from her fingers while she made smacking sounds.

"Must she do that, and if so can we go for that drive now?" Paul whispered in my ear.

Scarlet eyed him like a snake attempting to charm their prey right before attacking it.

"Mind your manners Paul. We are celebrating with Scarlet." I said.

It was my attempt at putting out a fire that Paul had just started.

"Oh is that what you call this?" He said.

Scarlet stood from her seated position and pranced in front of a huge gold plated mirror that adorned the wall. She flashed a smile at Paul and then at me and back at Paul again. That smile was one that I knew all too well and it spelled trouble. She made my heart hold still when she smiled with her teeth showing and no emotion.

"What is it Scarlet?" I asked worried but smiling back.

"Just thinking of a fitting gift for the two of you is all." She lied.

"A gift for what?" I asked.

"Your wedding silly. Maybe some sexy lingerie... I'm sure Paul would agree with that one?" She taunted while looking at me seductively.

Paul was quiet and sour. I knew that he wanted to leave and especially now that Scarlet was teasing him and being flirtatious with me.

"Well you have plenty time to think about that Scarlet." I said.

"Not really." Paul fought back.

Scarlet stared directly at him and then burst out laughing.

"What's so fucking funny?" Paul demanded while now standing and with a reddened face.

I grabbed his hand to settle him from an unmoved Scarlet.

She glowed and for a second her face turned serious and deadly. We all stood still and in silence as Scarlet's reflection disappeared for just a few seconds from the mirror next to her. Paul and I looked to the other for assurance or denial. I am still not certain which one. Only Scarlet knew of her intentions for allowing us to witness that, especially Paul.

"I am getting the fuck out of here." Paul said rushing to the door. He turned toward me. "You are welcome to come with me." He said.

I looked to Scarlet and she shrugged her shoulders while releasing a warm smile. I smiled back.

"I'll be back Scarlet, going for a ride with Paul in his new car."

"Yeah, I noticed that. Enjoy." She said walking toward me. "Good night Pierre." She yelled after Paul.

Scarlet made sure that we were standing right in front of her screened door when she kissed me goodbye. Scarlet's mouth was warmer than usual as she kissed me to mark her territory. I could see Paul's face filled with disgust as I approached his car to get in. He did not bother to wait and open the door for me. Paul simply waited for me to get in and as soon as I closed the door he drove off as if he were running for his life.

"Why do you allow her to kiss you like that Koral?" Paul asked.

I rolled my eyes while sucking my teeth at his ignorance.

"You continue to ignore our closeness Paul. She is like a sister to me"

"That what she has for you is perverted and not natural."

I tuned Paul out and imagined Scarlet taking me right then and there in front of the door while Paul watched from the streets. It was my only thought as Paul continued to fuss about Scarlet. He had totally forgotten about his proposal and my rejection of it.

Paul had drained me the night before with all his talk about us running away together. I would have to surely break his heart soon. I just did not know how much more of it I could take. I knew in my heart of hearts that Paul was not the person that I wanted to spend my eternity with. He actually disgusted me with all his negative talk toward the woman that I loved dearly. Paul just did not understand that Scarlet was for me what he wanted to be. Scarlet was the only reason that I held on to living after Nana died.

My world would be troubled and awfully lonely without Scarlet. She gave me adventure, love and laughter and so very much more.

I had being praying that living with Scarlet would eventually pay off. I was not asking for her hand in marriage or for her to do something impossible. I knew that I could not be a wife or mother if I stayed with Scarlet but she was worth the sacrifice. I just wanted to be loved and I wanted all of the love that Scarlet Rose Laveau had to give. If only she would truly see me and give me that chance. *You are driving me crazy woman.*

I heard a knock on the door as I lingered on the toilet after drying myself. I allowed my fingers to fondle my folds in memory of Scarlet's many caresses. The knock was loud and persistent but one that I would continue to ignore because I was not expecting any company. I soon heard Scarlet stumble out of bed. She was a little more than upset. She yelled foul language through the house at the determined knocker.

"This better be damn good." I heard Scarlet say at the door.
"Sheriff Ma'am." A female voice replied.

Scarlet threw back the door with such force that it hit the wall.

"Well what brings you back to my door?" Scarlet replied while opening the screen door.

I jumped up from the commode and pulled up my panties. I rushed to crack the bathroom door. It was the cop that Scarlet had told me about. She had come around to question Scarlet about some customer of hers. I wondered why she was back and if Scarlet was in any type of trouble. I sincerely hoped that everything would be okay as I continued to listen.

"How may I help you? Mrs. Brazil Tio it is?" Scarlet asked.

"Ms. will do. I see that you have a good memory Ma'am. I'm just following up here."

"Following up on what?"

"The Jessie French case. Do you recall anything odd about his behavior?" The officer said.

I watched Scarlet rub the sleep from her eyes and yawn in the cops face.

"Nothing other than being visibly upset over the fact that his soon to be bride would die of his hands." Scarlet taunted.

"Do you really believe in the stuff that you feed people Ms. Laveau? I mean, do you feel any responsibility for Mr. French's death?"

Scarlet rose up from resting on the door frame and placed her hands on her hips. I could only imagine the ice cold look that she must have given to the officer.

"Now do not go shooting the messenger. And what the hell do I have to feel guilt over? I tell the truth to truth-seekers. No need for any regrets Ms. Tio. How about you?"

"How about me what?" The officer asked annoyed.

Scarlet stared at her for a second and I knew that she was reading her. She leaned back against the door frame and laughed a bit before continuing to question the lady officer.

"Do you believe the shit that I tell people? Would you admit to being here for more than the sake of Mr. French? And here alone?"

It angered me a great deal when Scarlet flirted with other women and I was hoping that I was just taking what I was hearing the wrong way. I had to get a good look at this woman. It was clear to Scarlet that Officer Tio had other intentions. I needed to know just what they were. I stood near the window and peeped out the worn drapes at the officer. She eyed Scarlet with a certain passion that I knew all too well.

Officer Tio was built up like a man and solid as a rock. Her copper skin was smooth and polished beneath the sun. She was model gorgeous but not pretty. She had these spacious marbled color eyes that complemented her. I felt immediately threatened and wanted her away from Scarlet. Officer Tio nervously fondled the tight bun pinned to the back of her head as Scarlet took control of the conversation. Brazil Tio watched Scarlet with wonder and resentment.

This was too much to witness and I was green with envy and decided to let them be. I had to prepare for work and should not have been snooping in the first place. *Lord help me.*

I had to laugh at myself as I pulled on my uniform. No way would Scarlet go for a woman that looked like a man. She would definitely prefer a real man, and she already had a real woman in me. I looked myself over in the mirror. The white button down cotton blouse embraced my ample chest and the tan pencil skirt hugged me well. I knew that Scarlet admired my curves and that she thought me to be beautiful. I felt gorgeous in my toasted and flawless skin in that moment. I ran my hands through my short curls to give them some sort of direction. *Maybe I should let it grow out. Scarlet might like that.*

Chapter Eleven
Scarlet

Even in my sleep I could see what most could not hear. My world was strange and full of wonder atop of reality. It was not easy being different in a mostly uniformed world and a society dedicated to bullshit. Even if most believed in a supernatural world such as myself, they would never admit it. I had been called many things, from a witch to a voodoo queen and at times a devil worshipper. Folks judged me because I was born seeing what should not be they said. I did not believe in the devil and therefore it made me incapable of serving him. People continued to request my services even with all the bullshit that they talked about me.

Brazil Tio now believed what she had doubted about me. She assumed me to be a fraud and responsible for Jessie French's death on the account of giving out false information. She became intrigued and was now a loyal customer after I read her and told her of her own desires and pains. People should never assume what is truth based on what has been taught to them by another. Belief should come from experience only. I had experienced a lot in life and my truth came directly from knowing exactly that.

My body belonged to many and I was not its only occupant. I could not be responsible for the longings of a mind belonging to multiple personalities in need of being satisfied in different ways. My thoughts could be very impure and malicious and my appetite to satisfy my needs was enormous. Brazil Tio was what I desired at the moment and Officer Tio is what I planned to have. I could smell the women beneath the men on her. She slept with men for reassurance and protection. Brazil was like most people that were afraid to just be. They had to be what was tolerable and Brazil wanted to be accepted and acknowledged. She had worked hard to pull her weight in a man's world and did not want to lose her position because of her heart's desire. But I had plans to get me some of what she had to offer and she knew it too. I sat at the window watching her patrol car pull up alongside the curve of my street. Her body of armor step from it. I watched her remove her sunglasses and almost march up to my door. Officer Tio certainly looked as if she was on official business but she had come for a Tarot Card reading. I had so much more planned for her that day.

Brazil walked to my door with hesitation in her face, but that did not stop her from proceeding to knock. I allowed her to pound on the door as I stood behind the door and pretended to be too busy to answer. At her steadfast persistence, I finally opened the door and welcomed her into my home. Her eyes filled with wonder as she took in the view of my place. I let her look around a bit and then escorted her to the table and briefly exchanged courtesies with her.

"See anything you like?" I asked.

Brazil turned to me. "Maybe."

"Are you ready for this?" I said as I picked up the Tarot Cards.

"Ready when you are." She said quick and fear filled.

I laid the cards out before her and explained the meaning of them.

"How can a card of the Fool be anything but a representation of foolishness on my part?" Brazil asked while shaking her head.

"The Fool does not hide from the light because she is the light." I answered.

Brazil's forehead lined with trouble. "Meaning?"

"That she only wants to appear foolish about certain things in her life." I said.

"And why would I do that?"

"To protect yourself."

"I'm not afraid of anything." Brazil lied.

Brazil Tio was foolish about many things, even if she chose not to admit it. She was a fool for becoming a cop. She thought that it would gain her that source of security that she lost when her virginity was stolen away from her. Being raped as a teenager was a secret that she carried with her like a battle mark. Brazil felt as if she had been the only woman violated in life. One thing we must learn as women is that we were put here to fail and our success depends upon not accepting the bullshit. When you are hit, you must hit back harder and make damn sure that your target is down and will not be getting back up. I dared any man to take my pussy from me without my permission. I would slit his dick right down the middle and serve it to him.

I trapped Brazil's eyes with mine. "Now Officer Tio, do you truly believe what you tell yourself or is it that bullshit goes down easier than the truth?" I offered.

Brazil looked to me with new eyes and a renewed faith in something and in someone. She managed a smile that lifted my clit. I wanted to experience her and know how many times her heart beats while having an orgasm. A chill fell over my body before I could finish fantasizing about the woman before me. Every hair on my body stood at notice. Something or someone was standing close behind me and wanted my attention. No way in hell was I going to take my eyes off the warm body before me to give note to the cold one behind me. I ignored the strong and possessive presence of the intruder and continued to stalk Brazil with my eyes.

"You tell me what I am afraid of Madame Scarlet?"

"You are frightened of your abilities and for that reason you play it safe in life. You Brazil Tio, ignore that still small voice within your head that calls out to you to succumb to your inner desires."

"And what might those be genius?"

"Wanting to know what it feels like to let go and get high, to run around naked and harm someone who has wronged you. And most of all, you want to love a woman without fear."

Brazil's spacious eyes increased in size. "A woman huh?"

"Yes. Not that you have not already laid with one. You have not been able to love a woman as you want to because you are afraid of judgment from your people and your God."

Brazil sat back in the chair. She rested her body and gave me her full attention. She pushed her legs forward and loosened her smile. I had her at that moment and she was mine to do as I pleased. I wanted to know what her pussy smelled like and most of all I wanted to fuck a cop. I had a need to wipe the superiority from her face that had been chiseled in over the years and make her my sub for the day.

The sun was out and peeping in through every crack and hole lighting our way to one another. Brazil's eyes had little specks of gold dancing around in them. I removed the holder from my hair and allowed my scarlet locs to fall down. Brazil looked on in need and want. I planned to give her a show as I stood up and walked around the table to greet her. She reached up to molest my locs.

"It is the reason my mother named me Scarlet."

Brazil twirled my locs in her hand. "Scarlet huh?"

"Good damn thing my hair stayed red." I laughed.

"Very good thing." Brazil replied without joining me in my laughter. She was a serious one.

I stood right in her sight and permitted the sun to reveal my nude body through the flimsy dress that I wore. Brazil licked her lips with satisfaction as she sat and watched me. When I leaned in to reach for her, she grabbed my wrist with much force and pushed me away from her.

"Wait right there. I just want to look at you for a minute longer." She said while standing to remove her belt from her waist and tossed it on the table.

I was a bit shocked and then realized that she was determined to play the macho role. I allowed her to take the lead until I was ready to take it back. She sat back down on the chair while pulling me on to her lap facing her.

"You are a dangerous and beautiful woman, Ms. Laveau."
"I am as harmless as you make me Ms. Tio."

We sat in that same position staring down our souls and reading minds. Brazil would have a hard time reading mine, for I had blocked her. It would be easier for her to read my body language. My pussy was right there on her legs and soaking up her pants. I moved my face to the side of her head and placed my lips on her ear.

"Can you feel that?" I asked while whispering in her ear.

Just as Brazil was about to answer the front door flew open and in walked Koral just a talking. She was not supposed to be home for at least another four hours. Koral agape and bulged eyes said it all. I really did not appreciate her actions or the reason that she would have done anything other than leave us alone. She should have just gone to her room or any other room for that matter. I rolled my eyes and laid my face against Brazil's to whisper my intentions to her as Koral just stood as if she was paralyzed.

"Koral!" I yelled.

"Yyyes, Scarlet." She replied like some damn chamber maid.

"Don't just stand there. Where are your manners? Speak and leave please."

Koral shook her head as to shake herself back into reality. "I'm sorry, hello officer."

"Her name is Brazil." I answered before Brazil could.

Brazil cleared her throat. "Hello."

Koral rushed from the room as I started to slow grind on Brazil. She stopped me before I got started good.

"This is sort of awkward now. Maybe another time? I should really be getting back to work." She said with all seriousness.

I could not believe that this was happening to me. Why did Koral have to fuck up a good thing? I wanted to go and punch her in her head but I kept my cool. I batted my eyes at my new found thrill and poked out my lips before smiling at her.

"I'm sorry Brazil. Another time for sure and make it much sooner than later."

"You bet I will." She said smiling back.

I removed my soaked body from her lap and pulled her to her feet. We both looked down at the wet spot on her pants and started to laugh.

"So you do laugh." I joked.

Brazil smiled sincerely as I offered to wipe away the evidence from her uniform. She was still on duty and had to return to work. I excused myself to the bathroom to retrieve a wet cloth and returned to clean Brazil up.

"Now that should dry as good as new." I said while escorting Brazil to the door.

"I want to kiss you but I choose anticipation." She whispered in my burning ear.

"And I wait in urgency." I admitted.

My face reddened as I closed the door behind Brazil. I could not help but be angry with Koral for being an idiot. She would make up for my loss. My pussy was still aching and full of need. I surely hoped that Koral was not too upset. I heard the shower running in the bathroom and removed my dress. I walked right into the bathroom to join Koral in the shower.

Chapter Twelve
Koral

Everything in the house was exactly the way that the Laveaus' had left it. Scarlet had no interest in bringing the place up to date. She enjoyed reliving the many memories that had been created in her childhood home that now it belonged to her. I sat at the rounded glass kitchen table that had held many of our meals over the years. The yellow and green floral wallpaper still adorned the walls and the green faux tile remained on the floors. I stirred my coffee and continued taking in the view of the kitchen that had me feeling as if I were stuck in time.

I remembered when Scarlet's mom was known as the palm reader in the neighborhood. Most folks called her the good witch because she healed people and gave only hope to them and never condemnation. People would always leave with a smile on their faces even if they came troubled. Mrs. Laveau was a milky white lady and not the type that we were used to seeing with a black man. It surprised most people that they were a couple. She was a good mother to Scarlet and always overly tender with me. She would help us dress our dolls and have tea parties with us. Mrs. Laveau taught us how to jump rope and hula-hoop. She also read to us and took us on nature walks often. Most found it hard to believe that she had given birth to a child like Scarlet, one with such a devious heart and soul. Mrs. Laveau pretended that it wasn't true and that all was well with Scarlet. But Nana said that Mrs. Laveau kept Scarlet close because she knew that she had given birth to a bad seed. Nana was wrong about Scarlet though. She was curious but not evil. I spent enough time with Scarlet and her family to know that.

Nana was very appreciative of the time that the Laveaus took up with me when she was busy working. Nana also took up their slack with Scarlet when needed. Nana always knew that Scarlet had inherited her mother's fortunetelling skills. Only Nana had said that Scarlet's heart was robbed of what it needed to do right by such a gift. It was a powerful gift that was deadly in the wrong hands she had said.

I do remember the time Scarlet had talked me in to tricking Marshall Bawdier into doing something rather dangerous. Marshall Bawdier was a classmate of mine that lived two blocks over. She often tried to play with Scarlet and I but was only allowed if Scarlet said it was okay, which was not that often. One day Scarlet decided that Marshall would be the perfect person to scare the shit out of and I mean literally. Scarlet had placed several garden snakes in the tree house. She had me invite Marshall up to the tree house promising to share some homemade cookies. Marshall was delighted to be asked to play. She went up to the tree house all excited.

"Oh my God! Help me!" She screamed.

I never saw a ghost with a heartbeat before that day. Marshall went from yellow to pale white. She fell out the tree house backwards. The poor girl broke her arm and shitted on herself. Scarlet laughed at Marshall and called her a sissy girl. I knew better than to do that because Nana would have spanked my butt for such a thing. Though I could not go against Scarlet, and when she looked in my direction I smiled and laughed a little.

Marshall screamed in pain until Scarlet's father showed up. Mr. Laveau swooped Marshall up in his big arms and carried her home kicking and crying and smelling of shit. Scarlet made me swear and cross my heart while hoping to die by sticking a thousand needles in my eye that we knew nothing about the snakes.

Mr. Laveau came charging toward us after taking Marshall home. He ripped into Scarlet something awful.

"Hurting people is unacceptable Scarlet!" Mr. Laveau said while shaking his finger in Scarlet's face.

Marshall had told everything. She said that Scarlet had also laughed and called her mean names. Scarlet swore up and down that it was untrue but her daddy told her that it was not right to treat people like that.

"Oh Daddy. I didn't mean it. I'm sorry that Marshall got hurt." Scarlet lied and held on to Mr. Laveau's leg.

Scarlet finally confessed and then the tears started. That was enough for Mr. Laveau to feel bad and comfort Scarlet instead of punishing her. I would have never gotten away with something like that with my Nana. Nana would have switched me good with a nice sized stick and I would have thought twice before messing with Marshall Bawdier again.

No matter what Scarlet did, I could never go against her. She had always been there for me in a nurturing and loving way, even as a child. She filled the void of needing something more than Nana. I wanted and needed my mother at times or even a father would have done and Scarlet understood that. With as much love as Nana gave me, I craved a different kind of love and in Scarlet I found that. She was motherly to me but in a more tender way. Nana's love was tough because she wanted my eyes wide opened. She was a no nonsense type of woman and I enjoyed that about her.

I also wanted to be touched beyond the heart. I wanted my spirit to experience satisfaction and Scarlet did that for me. She would hold me and caress me and kiss me gently until I felt secure. We had to hide our behavior after the age of ten. Nana told the Laveau's that it was unnatural for us to keep up in such a way and that it was due time that Scarlet and I took separate baths. I was angry with Nana for not understanding a different kind of love, but I was too respectful of her to speak up to her at such an age. Scarlet and I had to start sneaking around with our affection. Although Mrs. Laveau still allowed us to bathe together, the kissing and the touching were forbidden. This only made the two of us more curious and pushed us to explore more things whenever we had the chance to do so.

I needed that affection from Scarlet. It helped me feel close to my mother for some reason. Scarlet knew so much about her, a lot more than what Nana had shared with me. The stories that Nana had told me of my mother still left me feeling empty and hopeless. I never really felt anything until Scarlet spoke of her. Scarlet would hold me tight and tell me stories of my mother after she left me with Nana.

Scarlet told me that Precious Baptiste regretted leaving me and had plans to send for me. The only thing that kept her from me was her death. Scarlet said my mother died crying out for me. She had told her killer that she had a beautiful brown baby at home that was depending on her to come back for her. That man looked my mother in her enchanting eyes and grabbed a hand full of her dark long curls and told her "Bitch you should have thought about that before you crossed me." He choked her unconscious and beat her something bad and then left her to die in an abandoned building where her body still remained unclaimed. I could literally sense the emotions my mother must have felt at that time. My heart went out to her and I wished like hell that Scarlet could change the past and future and not just see it. I was happy that Scarlet had told me the truth about my mother. It was so much better than believing that she was somewhere not giving a damn that I existed like Nana would have had me to believe.

I decided to leave for work early. The wind was blowing slightly and the sun had cooled down a lot. I wanted to check out a few gift shops before my shift started. I had befriended an older guy at work by the name of Gray. I am not sure if Gray was his real name or not but that is what he was called by everyone. It could have been that he had one seeing brown eye and one dead gray eye. He was a spooky looking fellow but had a heart of gold. I often confided in him during our breaks and appreciated his advice. It felt natural telling him of my troubles and he seemed quite sincere when listening and responding to me.

Gray was always bringing us little treats and telling us uplifting stories. I would make-believe that he was the grandfather that I never had. It was his birthday and we planned to surprise him with a cake and gifts. I wanted to make sure that I picked out something extra special just because of what Gray represented for me. It was not often that I got a chance to buy gifts for folks, especially now that Nana was gone. There was only Scarlet and Paul to gift. I was excited about shopping for Gray.

I grabbed an early bus and checked out a few shops next to my job. I had plenty of time to find something nice and appropriate. I thought about a tie for Gray but he did not seem like the type and I could not imagine him in a tie. I wondered if he was a lover of books since he knew so much, but then again it could have been wisdom and not intelligence.

As I walked down the sidewalks and peered into the gift shop windows I started to feel alive again. Nana's death had stolen something from me and for a moment I just did not know what I would do without her. I did know that I had to keep on living and that Nana would not want me moping around forever. I thought about Paul and if I wanted anything at all from him and how I needed to do something about that situation sooner than later. I did not know why he could not just live here and we continue to date. There was no real reason to get married. Although, I did want babies and Nana would just die all over again if I attempted it outside of wedlock. We lived in different times now and many women were having babies alone.

I had to make some real serious decisions concerning my life. Just at the moment I needed to be more focused on Gray's gift. I finally went inside a shop that sold handmade shaving kits. I settled on a nice pine wooden engraved box that held everything Gray would need for a clean shave. There was a waiting time for the engraving and so I went across the street for coffee and dessert. I sat outside of the café with my coffee to finish enjoying the cool air while waiting for Gray's gift to be completed.

I made a mental note to have a serious talk with Paul. He had asked me to spend time with him on my off day. I agreed, and so I would be seeing him that following day. It was time to be a woman and be serious about my future.

Work was busy as usual. The restaurant I worked at was always packed with tourists and locals. The salary was okay and the tips were great. I had regular heavy hitters that were more than generous at times. I knew that some had other motives that I was not particularly interested in.

My mind was usually on Scarlet and or my future. I was approaching twenty-six and had never really been responsible for anything but looking after Nana looking after me. My feet were aching and my legs were throbbing after only half a shift worth of work. I had to suck it up and continue to work. I thought maybe one day I could go back to school for nursing or something. There was no way that I was going to continue working like a slave for pennies. I did not want much from life but I wanted comfort and a place of my own if I could not have one with Scarlet.

I almost ran into a customer by not paying attention. My head was in the clouds and I was also reminiscing about walking in on Scarlet and Brazil.

"Damn Koral, is your head screwed on today?" Raleigh asked.

"I'm sorry Raleigh, didn't see you coming."

"Then maybe you need glasses woman. I was right there in front of you."

Raleigh was a regular and one of the not so generous tippers if you refused to flirt back with him. He gave no woman reason to flirt with him. He was way too lanky to be considered attractive. Never mind the fact that he wore the same shirt damn near daily and that his teeth were as yellow as a sunflower. I usually ignored his advances and bad breath. I just accepted the two dollar tips that he left as punishment after running me raggedy.

I never did understand that about folks. They come in and demand you wait hand and foot on them. Same folks would leave your table penniless or they would leave pennies. Folks had to know that we made most our salary from tips. That was another reason that I would have to find a better job sooner than later.

I worried myself half to death with what Scarlet saw in Brazil Tio that she did not see in me. I mean, yeah, she had a career and all, but so what, I knew just how to please Scarlet and she was a hard one to please. I just prayed that there was something I could do to make her love me and me only. I wondered if Officer Tio's captain knew that she was trying to sex the citizens instead of protecting and serving them justly. I would find a way to persuade Scarlet into knowing that I was the only one for her. I knew what it would take to prove myself. It would take a whole lot of guts to pull it off and would go against my beliefs. But someone had to die soon before I lost my dream woman to a fictitious man.

At the end of my shift I cleared my tables and then helped clean up the rest of the restaurant. We had a mini celebration with Gray afterwards and toasted the occasion with Holy Ghost Punch. It was a traditional drink that was usually served for brunch and or the holidays. The Holy Ghost Punch was a favorite of Gray's and the reason that it was served. I loved the milky sweetness of it and how well it masked the taste of alcohol but snuck up on you without notice. I was feeling good too and would have had more, but I had to make it home in one piece.

After our small and quick celebration, Gray and I sat outside waiting on our rides. Gray's wife picked him up and Paul had been picking me up since he got his car. It was nice not having to ride the bus all the time, but I did not appreciate waiting either. He was well aware of the time that I got off. I just hope he was not somewhere goofing off while I waited. Paul had better have a good ass reason for leaving me waiting. I was not really all that mad because I enjoyed my time with Gray and his wife Odessa was always late and never apologetic. They were so cute together though, both being petite in stature with huge personalities. Gray never complained about her being late either, or at least not that I knew of.

"Gray, may I ask you a question?"
"Yes um." Gray said.

He looked straight at me while he put his cigarette out beneath his foot. I hesitated not knowing if I should be so nosey.

"How come you never complain about being picked up late when your wife does not work anywhere?"
"I ain't in no hurry for nothing. She get here when she get here. One less thing to fuss about."
"I guess I should not be in a hurry either huh?" I said.

Gray took a long hard look at me. "You young, you will be fast to do things and slow to learn, but you find out sooner than later to just be still and watch in front of you before it sneaks up behind you and steal your breath away."

I thought about what all that meant and then continued to speak.

"I won't be young forever and I have so much I want to do." I said while letting my heart linger on visions of Scarlet.

"One would assume you were speaking of that yellow fellow that scoops you up, but your heart beat faster when you mention her."

Gray startled me with that accusation but it was one that I could not deny. And before I could question him more about his thoughts his wife Odessa pulled up like a bat out of hell. She blew the horn several times as if we were not sitting right there in front of her. I helped Gray to the car with his gifts and leftover cake.

"Hey Mrs. Odessa." I said while handing Gray his gift bags.

"Humph. Gray hurry up, I ain't got all night for you to be out here flirting." Odessa complained without acknowledging me.

"You gone be okay out here by yourself?" Gray asked with Odessa still fussing in the background and threatening to pull off.

"Yeah, you better go ahead." I said laughing beneath my breath.

I stood against the cold brick wall wrapping my overcoat around me and searched the streets for any sign of Paul. Just when I was about to walk down to the phone booth and call a cab Paul shows up skinning and grinning. He jumped out the car to run around and open my door.

"Baby I am sorry. I had a gig that went over but the money was well worth it, more money for our big move."

"Gig? I thought you were done with that." I said rolling my eyes.

"One time thing a dude asked me to do for his parents' anniversary. The original entertainment pulled out on him last moment. But he paid us good baby."

I was half listening and extra tired.

Paul was talking as if I had agreed already. I decided not to acknowledge it and just be grateful for the free ride. Gray was right, good things came to those who had the patience to wait on them.

"Why are you so quiet Koral? How was your day?"

"Just a lil tired is all. My day was challenging and I'm just glad that it is over. How about you Paul?"

"Can't complain, can't complain, happy to be with you now." He replied with that never ending grin attached to his face.

I was hoping that Paul would not have much to say. I wanted to maybe listen to the radio and enjoy a quiet drive home but did not want to seem rude by asking. I could tell that he had something on his mind and either wanted to stay the night or wanted to do something with me. I really was not up for the company and did not want to continue sneaking him into Scarlet's house without her permission. I needed to let her know that Paul had been coming over and ask if it was okay with her. I felt like I had been being disrespectful by allowing him to climb through the window. I no longer lived with Nana and I was not some teenage girl fooling around behind her mother's back anymore. I was a full grown woman with needs just like the next woman. I am sure Scarlet would not mind, but then again it was Paul, she just might.

Either way I needed her permission before I allowed it again and so I would just tell him I was too tired if he asked.

"What you smiling so about Paul?"

He turned to face me briefly before putting his eyes back on the road. "You are off tomorrow right?"

"Yes."

"You mind me taking this pretty little lady I know on a picnic in the park?"

I bent my face up. "It is a lil chilly for a picnic."

"Maybe so, but I'll keep you warm Koral and it is not that cold til later in the evening. Come on and say yes woman. I already bought the wine."

I thought for a moment and I had no real reason to say no. I decided to make his night.

"I think a picnic would be nice." I said with a gentle smile. After all, I needed to get out and enjoy myself.

Paul smiled even harder and then requested to stay over in which I turned him down flat. You give Paul an inch and he took a yard. All I wanted was a quick shower and a bed to myself and if it was not asking too much a moment with or even a glimpse of Scarlet before calling it a night. I prayed that she did not have Brazil over. I just wanted the two of us in the house and not a third wheel. In my mind she belonged to me and had always belonged to me. I was not about to let Brazil step over me and take Scarlet away without a fight. I planned to surprise her tomorrow by bringing up us killing someone together all on my own. I did not want to take somebody's life away just because and I really did not understand Scarlet's obsession with it, but I was willing to do any and everything that she requested because of the love that I had for her.

I lay in bed that night listening to Scarlet and that Brazil woman carry on like two wounded animals. Scarlet had to know that I could hear her and I almost made myself believe that she was purposely being extra loud to make me jealous. I tossed and turned trying my best to fall asleep and push the thought of Brazil's hands and mouth all over Scarlet out of my head. *This sucks so much.*

Scarlet was screaming out Brazil's name as if she were God in the flesh, which made my stomach turn. I turned my radio on. It was the same one that Nana used to listen to. I hoped that the music would block out the noise. Scarlet's moans seeped through the music and I had to place my pillow over my head.

I felt this wetness on my face and realized that I was crying. I just hated having to be present for that. I always knew that Scarlet was sexually active with other people but I was never really exposed to it. She had asked me on many occasions to have a threesome with her and I had agreed but it just never happened for one reason or another. I wanted so much to be the one she loved on that night. But the only thing I was able to hold on to was a pillow and a quilt.

Maybe I should have allowed Paul to come over that night. At least then I could have had something to ease my mind just a little. And maybe I would have made noises in hopes of making Scarlet just as jealous. But I knew I could never make her jealous of Paul. She just detested him because he was Paul and it had nothing to really do with me. She would have hated him even if we were not dating.

I guess I had no right to be jealous when I had Paul and all. But I only had Paul because I could not have Scarlet all the time. She thought it was best that I dated other people and not devote all my attention to her.

Scarlet had refused to see me for weeks once because she felt like I was suffocating her and wanted me to find somebody else to occupy my time. So I took Paul up on his offer after he continuously begged me for a date. He picked up on my feelings for Scarlet right away and her hold on me and decided that he hated her just as much as she hated him. I finally fell asleep just to wake up to repeated sounds of Scarlet and Brazil making out. I prayed that it was only sex and nothing more. My heart depended on it. *Dear God, if you still love me, please do not let Brazil take Scarlet away.*

"Oh Brazil…Brazil, Brazil…" Scarlet cried out into the night.
"Please God."

The sun was blazing in the clear blue sky and the grass was still slightly green. Nothing could mask the cold that was steadfastly approaching us. Paul insisted on having a picnic in the park despite the cool temperature. I could not afford to get sick and made sure to cover my body well. I wore baby blue legwarmers over blue jeans and a white sweater with a scarf to match. My hair had begun to grow out and had no particular style, just curls on top of curls.

Paul and I sat up under one of the mature live oaks in City Park. It was a beautiful tree filled with hanging moss. It shielded us from most of the sun, except for the drops of light that peeked through the leaves and moss to expose us. Paul was facing me and mumbling something that I wasn't ready to hear just yet. I was taking in the splendor of the park and the many people that were there. They appeared to be just as quiet as I was. Maybe they were in awe of the park as well or just maybe I had tuned them out along with Paul.

I remembered when the Laveau's would bring Scarlet and I to City Park. We would play hide-and-go-seek. Mr. Laveau was always the seeker because he was too big and tall to hide from us. Sometimes I wished that we could go back to those simple times and just be free again with no responsibilities other than to just enjoy life. Who wanted to grow up just to have the world on your back trying to beat you back in the ground or make you marry just to try and survive the inevitable.

"Koral, are you with me?" Paul asked waving his hand in front of my face.

"I'm sorry, just got caught up in memories." I said and tried to pay attention.

With that, Paul went back to talking and I went back to not listening but observing the beautiful man that sat before me. Paul was so gorgeous that I knew men had to want him as well. The thought made me wonder if he had ever been with a man. It would remain a thought because there was no way that I would have asked such a thing. Suddenly the Miniature Train passed by blowing its horn and grabbing my attention away from its accusations of Paul. I clapped and laughed in delight and memory of fun times on that very train.

"Would you like to ride?" Paul asked sitting there all radiant in his tan slacks and red sweater vest over a blue stripped button down cotton shirt. He always managed to dress and smell good. I wished Paul was as mentally satisfying as he was physically. I could surely spend my whole life enjoying his splendor. But what kind of life would that be when my heart alone would be with Scarlet. I finally decided to tune into what Paul was saying and give him half a chance to give me one good reason why I should ever leave New Orleans and Scarlet behind.

"Earth to Koral." Paul said teasing.

"I'm listening." I lied.

"Maybe, but you're not answering. How about a train ride?"

"Naw, not now at least. Let us just talk. I would like some wine though." I said smiling.

Paul had a nice spread laid out for us. A soft red and white checkered blanket adorned with different types of cheese, luscious grapes, and Muffaletta and Po'boy sandwiches. There were also strawberries and Sangria. Paul was really laying it on thick and I sort of liked being courted. He uncorked the wine and poured me a half glass full.

"Here you are my lady." Paul teased in a proper tone.

I leaned over to kiss him on the cheek while accepting the wine. "Thank you Paul, you have been good to me."

"My plans are to always be good to you." He said.

I smiled before falling victim to my thoughts of Scarlet again. She had also been good to me and for a lot longer than Paul. I recalled the time that we played in the sprinklers in the Laveau's backyard. We ran in and out from the sprinklers getting soaking wet. My hair was then long but never as long as Scarlet's. The wetter we got the more our body parts were exposed through our summer dresses. Scarlet soon initiated carnal comments. We were barely sixteen and she was speaking to me in an adult way and my body was responding womanly. It was unlike our exploring times. Scarlet told me what she wanted to do to me in whispers because the Laveau's sat on the steps half watching us and reading the paper.

"I wish I could kiss your breast right now, right here,"

Scarlet teased before running in the house and cueing me to follow her. The Laveau's laughed at our childish behavior and were delighted that we still seemed childlike at such an age. Mr.

Laveau would always tell us that there was no reason to rush growing up and he continued to buy us dolls and bags of candy well into our teenage years.

Once we reached Scarlet's room she turned on me. "Shut and lock that door behind you." She demanded. I did as she asked and when I turned around she was standing in front of me. Her locks of red hair were dripping of water and her face was serious with suggestions. Scarlet allowed her sundress to fall to the floor. She stepped over it and allowed her body to press up against mine. I was a little intimidated and scared at the same time because the Laveau's were right out back. Scarlet could care less as she brushed her lips across mine and whispered her devotion to me.

"I will always love you." She whispered.

Fear was not enough to keep me from accepting love from the love of my life. Scarlet had taught me all that I knew about love and I would always be open to learning more.

"Koral, Koral…Koral." Paul repeated to get my attention.

"Yes Paul?" I answered while sipping the wine and picking up a strawberry to play off ignoring him again.

"I'm starting to feel like I am on this date all alone. Where are you right now?"

"I'm here Paul, just lost in memories." I said while stretching out my legs to change the subject.

Paul's eyes traveled the length of my long figure as I knew they would. I sat my glass down and enjoyed another strawberry while watching Paul watch me. It was easy getting his mind to take a detour. I removed my scarf that once belonged to Nana from around my neck and tossed it at Paul. He adored my long neck. I teased my curls while licking my lips. Paul came closer to trace my neck before teasing it with his warm mouth. It felt good but not as good as it was when Scarlet did it. She was like a serpent that got inside of you and wreaked havoc on your mind, body and soul at the same time.

"Oh Scarlet my love." I whispered into Paul's ear and before I had time to realize what I had done Paul was on a rampage.

He moved away from me. "Scarlet? What the fuck do you mean by calling me that whore's name?"

I gathered my thoughts before pretending as if I were clueless. "What is the matter Paul?"

"You know damn well what the matter is! You called me Scarlet and I demand to know why?"

"I do not recall saying that and even if I did, it is no reason for you to behave this way or call my best friend out of her name. I will not tolerate it!"

"Best friend my ass. You love that woman like you supposed to love me."

"I do love her… so what?"

"Do not pretend that you did not see that evil bitch disappear from the mirror. Something is really wrong with her Koral."

Paul was going too far and even if I did see her disappear why did it have to equate to evil and magical?

"I saw no such thing Pierre DePaul!"

"The quicker you get away from here and her the sooner you can come to your senses and know that you cannot live that kind of sinful life."

"Do not preach to me Paul! You know not what you speak of. Scarlet is like a sister to me. And yes we are closer than most, but do not think for a moment that you know our story dammit!"

I snatched up my scarf and headed out of the park toward Paul's car while yelling behind me.

"Take me home now!"

I sat in the car watching Paul kick around our picnic stuff before throwing it all in the basket and marching over to the car like a kid having a tantrum. He could be so cute but I was damn mad with him at the moment. Not because he called me out but because of his hatred for Scarlet. Paul opened his car door and threw the picnic basket in the backseat before jumping into the front seat and slamming the car door. I ignored him by looking straight ahead and keeping my arms folded around me.

"I'm sorry Koral, I just get fucking mad over the hold that witch has on you." Paul said turning to me and waiting on a response.

He would not be getting one because he insisted on berating my dear friend and lover. When he did not get a response from me he sped out of the park and down the street right past a patrol car. I just knew the police would get behind us soon, but it never did happen.

Once we reached Scarlet's place, Paul attempted to get out and open my door.

"No, don't bother getting out. Just go home Paul, I will manage fine." I said opening the car door and stepping out.

"Koral baby please, I ain't mean nothing by it, I am just a man with his heart in your hands, Can you understand that baby? Just a jealous old man."

I didn't feel like his begging and I knew he would continue if I did not end it quick.

"Maybe tomorrow you can think of a way to make it up to me but not today. Go on now before I change my mind."

Paul smiled big and bright. "Yes ma'am." He replied while tipping a pretend hat and driving off.

Chapter Thirteen
Scarlet

It was a mighty dark night. The street lights seemed rather dim and unaccommodating. Maybe my physical sight was failing me, but there was something strange about that night.   Something was stirring and that something was determined to make its mark. I was about three blocks away from home, cold and ready to settle down into a warm bath. I walked with desperation and maybe even a bit of hunger. I had been across town visiting a spirit house and stayed longer than I had planned. The bus was taking too long to show and I did not want to spend unnecessary money on a cab when a brisk walk would get me home.

As I approached my home, I noticed Pierre's car sitting on the curb right in front of my property. I wondered what the hell he was doing there. Koral should have still been working and had a while before she would be off. Pierre was well aware of Koral's schedule. Then I started thinking that maybe Koral had gotten off earlier than expected. Though the house was dark and her man was sitting outside my house parked. He appeared to be the only one in the car, but maybe her face was in his lap. I let my mind run wild until I approached Pierre's car and found him alone and dozing. I just did not understand what Koral saw in the dude. Maybe some pretty babies but that was about all he could probably manage.

"Pierre?" I said in an emotionless tone.

He rubbed the sleep from his eyes and stared at me as if I had two heads. He sat up.

"Hey Scarlet. Um we got off on the wrong foot the last time and I wanted to apologize for being less than the gentleman that I am." He said.

I laughed a bit. "And you are here for that?"

"Yes and no."
"I thought so." I said about to walk off.

Pierre turned around and reached for something in his backseat before facing me again.

"Well now Scarlet, I did come to say I'm sorry. But I also wanted to know if you would put these flowers and this gift box in Koral's room for me? I sure would appreciate it. If it was not a surprise I'd give it to her myself."

Pierre was so pathetic. I thought to tell him hell no, but something pushed me into responding out of the ordinary.

"No Pierre, I cannot do that…"
"But Scarlet…"
"Now hush a second and let me finish will you. You can do it yourself."

Pierre looked at me and allowed his mouth to hang open.

"You are going to let me in?" Pierre said with disbelief.
I chuckled. "Why not? You been sneaking through the window in the middle of the nights anyhow."

Pierre looked ashamed and blushed very womanly before thanking me and leaping from the car to follow me through the already opened gate. As we stepped up on the porch, I turned to look back at him and shook my head at the stupidity etched in his face. Once inside, I stood aside to allow him entrance. He hesitated at his reflection in my eyes but moved swiftly shortly after.

I closed the door behind me just to turn and find Pierre standing as stiff as a soldier.

"Hurry along. I don't have all night you know." I said startling him into action.

"Thank you again Scarlet." Pierre said walking towards Koral's bedroom.

"Don't keep thanking me, just do what you came for and get out."

"Yes ma'am."

Pierre was so ridiculous, I could hardly stand it. I went to the kitchen to pour myself a glass of bourbon to warm and relax my cold and tired body. I filled my glass and I imagined a perfect night. A night where I fell asleep satisfied and well fed and not from food but from deed. I reached for a second glass and filled it as I returned from the kitchen in just enough time to reach Pierre before he opened the front door to leave.

"Hey, I did not want to be rude and only pour myself a glass, and hell I owe you an apology as well."

Pierre looked stunned as he twisted the knob. "Thanks but no thanks." He said while shaking his head and grinning.

He was so damn suspicious of me. How could Pierre call himself a man and be afraid of little ol' me?

"No seriously, I do this for the love of Koral. She is like a sister to me and I want her happiness. If that includes you, so be it. We may as well start making it work and if not with love then with respect?" I said raising the glass to him again.

Pierre's eyebrows rose to his hairline and then he slowly allowed a smile to form before reaching for the glass. I wondered if I could truly fuck him without barfing or having heart failure. I knew for sure that I could probably get him into bed, but what would that gain me? Maybe it would guarantee him being removed from my life with or without Koral.

"So, are you picking Koral up tonight?"

"Yes, of course." He said looking at me as if it were a dumb question.

I plotted as I made small talk with the slightly shaking Paul. We talked about his plans to take Koral away and make a family in some beautiful suburban place. Pierre had big dreams and I guess he was on to something. He did have that nice car sitting outside. Though there was no way that Koral would be happy with just Pierre. He would certainly have to have a fool proof plan in mind. I went to fill Pierre's glass again as he continued to talk bigger than his pockets. Only this time I added a little something special.

I returned with pound cake and more bourbon. Pierre reached for two slices of cake but refused the bourbon. I shook my head while sucking on my teeth and moved the glass in his direction.

"I usually would not refuse a drink but I do have to drive to get Koral." Pierre lied with caution.

"Sure a big strong man like yourself can handle a second glass and still drive a car with perfection."

Pierre's ego flared up and he took the glass and damn near swallowed it whole. He placed the goblet on the coffee table.

"I'm going to head to the toilet before leaving if that's okay with you Ms. Scarlet."

"Why so early? You still have two hours before picking up Koral."

"I'm going to fetch some dinner at her workplace and wait while she cleans up."

"I see." I said

"Well thanks for the drinks and cake." Pierre said as he shut the bathroom door behind him. I could hear him pissing and it sounded like a damn waterfall. He walked right out the bathroom and the bastard had not even bothered to wash his hands.

I sat looking at him in disgust but disguised it with a false smile.

"All done?"

"Yes ma'am." He said approaching the door and bracing his now unstable body up against it.

Pierre looked to me with a dazed face before attempting to lunge at me. I quickly moved out of the way of his falling body. He hit the floor with a loud thump and began to crawl in my direction. I looked all around me before running to the kitchen to retrieve the bottle of bourbon. I returned with urgency and with all my might I hit Pierre across the head knocking him all the way out. I checked his pulse and it was steady. In remembrance of Nana I rushed to Koral's room to get a pillow from her bed. I made sure to grab a pillow that was used for decoration and not for sleeping. When I returned to the living room I stood over Pierre with a beating heart. It was not one of fear but a pounding of power.

Once the pillow was over Pierre's head I straddled him and pushed with all my might. His arms suddenly reached for me and gripped my shoulders with a short lived source of strength. His nails dug into me and made long scratches on my arms as they traveled to their death. *Die bitch die.* Pierre was quiet for eternity now and he would be no more. I removed the pillow and held his eyelids back. Those beautiful eyes of his were now rolled into the back of his head. I smiled and closed them back. I returned the pillow to Koral's bed. I used her pillow to show my affection toward her. It was only fitting to give her his last breath since I had taken him away from her.

Pierre's murder had been an easy kill. One not planned or thought out. There was no blood or guts spilled all over the place. But he did have this big ass lump halfway up his forehead leading to the top of his head. The lump was red as an apple and swelled by the second. *What the fuck am I supposed to do with this body?*

I dialed Brazil's number after carefully considering whether or not to involve another person. I thought about Momma and Daddy Laveau and how it would hurt them dearly to ever see their beloved daughter in the midst of any trouble and especially murder. I had to know for sure that Brazil was the right person to reach out to. Koral had flaked on a couple of occasions and I just did not know how she would react to me murdering Pierre. I could not trust her to hold up if something went down and the police got involved. Although I felt that she was more dedicated to me than she was to Pierre, I just couldn't risk my liberty on a maybe.

The phone rang about two times before I got an answer. "Brazil speaking."

I fell silent and held the phone breathing deeply and then sobbed lightly as Brazil asked who was calling repeatedly. I pretended to hesitate before I finally responded.

"It is me. Scarlet." I said softly.
"Is everything okay?"
"No… it is not. And I am so sorry but I did not know who else to call. I feel so all alone and so very afraid right now." I cried with as much sincerity as I could muster up.
"What has happened?" Brazil asked with concern.

"Can I trust you before I speak?"

"Yes… of course you can." She answered with a bit of reluctance.

"I need to know that I can trust you with my life. Once I tell you this, there will be no turning back. I know that we have only just met but I feel so very strongly towards you and that's the only reason that I decided to reach out to you."

"I feel it too and I have been thinking of you all day. So just tell me Scarlet."

"Good… I am glad to hear that." I said. Do you think you can come over… it is too awful to speak about over the phone like this." I continued.

"Give me ten minutes and I will be there."

"Please hurry. I'm so afraid." I lied.

I rushed about my place knocking a few things over and made certain to return one goblet to its rightful place after cleaning it. I threw the other to the floor, breaking it near Pierre's body. I pressed my hands down into the glass cutting them up slightly and took a piece of the glass to make a few small flesh cuts aside my face. *You best make it look good.* I continued to bite down on my lower lip and punched the side of my face. My dress was torn slightly to expose my breast and I released my hair from its holder. My eyes were cried out and red from the sheer passion that burnt within my soul. I could make no mistakes with Brazil. I needed her on my side.

Minutes later, Brazil was outside my door knocking. I looked to Pierre who was just lying there dead. I thought of how I should have unzipped his trousers and pulled them down, but I did not want to chance moving his body. I made my way to open the door for Brazil and fell right into her arms.

Brazil looked horrified and concerned."What the hell happened to you?" Brazil asked pulling me away from her to take a look at me.

I slowly backed into the house and allowed her to enter and witness the scene in full view. Brazil gasped for air and placed her hand over her mouth. She looked to me perplexed and then ran to Pierre dropping to her knees to check him for any signs of life.

"Who is this man Scarlet and what the fuck happened here?" She questioned.

Forcing the tears to continue I answered between sobs.

"This man used to be my roommate Koral's boyfriend."
"Well, where is Koral and why is he here dead on your floor woman?"

I paced the floor while telling Brazil how Pierre had wanted to come in and leave a gift for Koral only to attack me. I told her how I had fought for my life and almost lost before I spotted the bottle of bourbon on the coffee table and managed to grab it to defend myself.

"I did not realize that I had hit him so hard. I did not want to kill him… I just wanted him to stop hurting me is all."
"I have to call this in Scarlet."
"No one will believe me because Pierre and I had no love lost between us." I cried out to her.
"What do you expect me to do then? They will believe you and I can say that I overhead most of it on the phone." Brazil advised.
"Oh God Brazil! That will not work. I cannot tell my best friend that I killed the man that she was about to marry. Koral just lost her grandmother. This would surely kill her. Please help me."

"Then what will you tell her Scarlet? What do you want from me? I am an officer of the law."

I looked to her with wide eyes. The same look I gave Daddy Laveau to get my way.

"I know and I apologize for dragging you into this but I had no one else. Brazil please help me. I was thinking that we could just get rid of the body and make this all go away somehow."

Brazil came to me and fondled my bruises before gathering me in her arms where I sobbed for my life and her understanding. I did not know what I would do if she did not help me and decided to call in Pierre's murder. I would have to have a second plan. There was no way that I would do time for killing his sorry ass. The world would not miss him and Koral had no real desire to marry him anyhow. I could not forget the many times he had disrespected me and my name. I just wondered what the bastard's last thoughts were. I camouflaged my smile with pleading eyes as I reached for Brazil's lips with mine. She kissed me briefly before deciding to help me.

"Have you looked at yourself? Your roommate will know something has happened to you and when is she due home?"

"I have makeup to cover it and will explain anything else that is noticed as an accident. Koral does not really question me like that. She will be off in less than two hours and will have to make it home still."

"I see. This is crazy you know and I could lose my job. You had better be worth it." She said with love filled eyes.

Brazil sat down on the sofa and looked from me to Pierre and back again before lowering her head into her hands. She stayed that way for a little longer than I found to be comfortable. I tried to question her about her silence but Brazil only ignored me and so I sat quietly across from her and waited it out.

"Okay Scarlet. I need you to listen carefully and do everything I tell you and do not fuck up at all. Do you understand?" Brazil demanded while removing her uniform.

"Yes!" I replied not understanding why she was getting undressed at such a time.

I hope that she does not want me to fuck her before helping me. I would much rather remove Pierre's body before Koral arrived home.

"Put on my uniform. And is that Pierre's car parked out front?"

"Yes but…"

"No buts just fall into action please."

Brazil's take charge attitude was very appealing to me. I did as she said because it stimulated me to do so.

Brazil removed Pierre's shirt and pants and retrieved his car keys from his pocket. She got dressed in Pierre's clothing.

"I need some plastic bags, a blanket and some duct tape."
I moved as quickly as I could.

I gathered her request and helped her to place Pierre's body in plastic bags before rolling him up in the blanket and securing it with duct tape. Brazil said that we would have to hide the body in the house for tonight and get rid of it tomorrow night because there was no time to do it all before Koral came home.

We hid Pierre's body beneath my bed and pushed it all the way back to the wall and placed my shoe boxes in front of him. Koral was not a snoop and so I was not really worried about her going through my things.

We cleaned up the front room and got rid of any evidence that Pierre had been there or that there had been a struggle. I was falling fast for Brazil. I loved the many sacrifices that she had made for me. I could not wait to show her my appreciation after all of this was over.

"Damn! I forgot to ask, can you drive?" Brazil said with concern.

I looked at her as if she had lost her mind. "Yes, my daddy taught me before I was twelve." I responded with a bit of pride.

"Good. Grab a change of clothes and let's go. You get in my car and follow me while I drive Pierre's." Brazil demanded. She was really good at this.

We left my house in the middle of the night on a mission that only Brazil knew of. I followed her as instructed. We drove to an old abandoned building and parked Pierre's car after wiping it down for fingerprints. Brazil got in the car with me and we changed into our own clothing. She placed Pierre's clothing in a bag and told me to place them with his body until the next night.

"Never speak of any of this to anybody. Do you understand? No matter what they say, Pierre was never in your house."

"Yes I understand." I said to a nervous but aware Brazil. She grabbed my face and focused in on my eyes. "Repeat it."

Her warm hands ignited me. "Pierre was never in my house."

"Even if someone spotted his car, you never saw him tonight."

I sighed heavily. "I understand Brazil."

"Oh and I need you to do one thing. Do not ask any questions yet, just do this. Tomorrow go out and buy cement mix." She continued.

Why in the hell did she want me to buy cement mix?
"Cement mix?"

Now she sighed as well. "Yes Scarlet. We are going to build a sidewalk in your backyard. Now please… no more questions." She said sarcastically.

"I owe you my life." I said tearfully.

"Damn right you do." Brazil said before looking to me.

"Are you okay Scarlet? I'm so sorry this had to happen to you."

"I will be, thanks to you." I said and laid my head on her shoulder.

Brazil smiled and drove me home and stayed with me for a while. She had planned to stay until late in the night when we were sure that Koral was asleep. She wanted to make sure that I was okay and also be a barrier between Koral and I. Koral would not visit my room if I had company. And I needed to avoid her that night to gather my thoughts.

Sleeping over Pierre's body gave me a sense of control like never before. No way could I allow Brazil to think for one moment that I was anything but frightened out of my mind. While I trusted her with my secret, she was not ready for me to reveal my appetite for murder to her. It was an ache that was embedded in my heart and soul. I had no idea where it came from. All I knew is that the desire for it plagued me night and day. I felt like a Lioness in hunt of prey.

My urge for killing would increase with everything that I watched die. I remembered when my pet bird died. I knew that I could have saved it if I wanted to. Poor thing was just trapped and needed to be set free. I was more interested in watching it suffer from a lack of care and the inability to get what it needed. My thoughts scared me for a second but then I felt it foolish to be afraid of self. I could not ignore my desires any more than I could have changed how I came into the world.

I loved because I was expected to love not because I felt all warm and tingly like my parents had explained to me. There was never any type of sensation in my heart for anything or anyone. The only thing that throbbed in my body was my clit when it wanted liberty from the desire that had crept up inside of it from being turned on by a body that I was attracted to. My attraction had nothing to do with love and everything to do with a desire. I did love my parents and Koral in my way, a way that was more a form of perfection than one of love. They protected me too. Even when they knew things about me that would send others running away from me. In return for their dedication to me, I gave them my trust and that was as close to love as I could get.

I laid there embraced in Brazil's arms wanting to make out with her. I could smell her and wanted her essence in my mouth. She would think me to be a lunatic if I tried to screw her with Pierre's body under my bed. Then again, I just might find out something new about Brazil Tio. After all, she had helped me so far and this was no easy task for anyone to get tied up in and especially not a cop, of all people.

I wondered how we would get rid of Pierre's body but I also knew not to push Brazil by questioning her so soon. She said that we would take care of it and I trusted that we would do so. I fell asleep with thoughts of how possible it was for me to grow comfortable having Brazil in my world.

The next evening after dark Brazil shows up with sulfuric acid and perennial flower seeds. I looked toward her in confusion. *What the fuck is all of that. Let's get this Negro from beneath my bed before he starts smelling.*

"Don't fret Scarlet. I don't see how it would be safe trying to carry a big ass body without bringing some attention to us from your nosey neighbors." Brazil said reading my mind.

"Do you feel it is any safer keeping him here?"

"Yes. I had a fellow that owed me big get a hold of enough acid to cover the body in. The acid will dissolve the body completely.

Brazil wanted to dig a grave and put Pierre's body in it. She said that we would cover the body with acid and then cement it over before covering it back up with dirt. Once the ground was replaced we would make flower beds in that disturbed part of the ground.

I was a little hesitant. "Are you serious?"

Brazil rushed past me and continued talking. "Yes, and I want you to go out tomorrow and get more flower seeds. I was only able to get the one bag tonight. I did not have time to figure out which flowers to plant in the fall season."

"I am going to trust you on this." I said while leaning in for a quick kiss."

We dug a grave seven feet deep because seven was my lucky number. Paul's body along with any evidence of him or the acid being there was placed down in a plastic barrel that I usually used to collect leaves off the ground in the fall. The acid was poured in and the lid was placed on the barrel and sealed numerous times with electric tape. The barrel was put down in the ground and cement was placed over it. We refilled the earth with its contents and planted a garden of Perennial's in the disturbed and exposed area. I would plant more flowers in the surrounding areas the next day to give it an oval design and purpose to the look. And as Brazil had promised, she poured out a side walk leading from the steps to the garden.

I held on to her and wanted to give her all of my appreciation right then and there but we were both dirty and a bit chilly. Right around the time Koral's shift ended at work Brazil and I had completely finished our mission. We had enough time to get cleaned up and be posted up in my bedroom by the time Koral arrived home. I was hoping that I would not have to continue acting like a victim for too long. I was longing to show Brazil my gratitude.

Chapter Fourteen
Koral

It was so unlike Paul to just leave me at work late at night like that. He had not called to explain his no show and had not been by the house or my job in days. I knew deep down in my heart that something had to be wrong. Paul would not leave me stranded at work in the middle of the night without reason. When I could not reach him by phone, I went by the rooming house that he called home.

Paul's landlord claimed to not have seen or heard from him either. All kind of thoughts went through my head. Perhaps he gave up on me when I decided to call him Scarlet while we were necking. I wanted to believe that maybe he had grown tired of begging me and decided to move on without me. Only my heart would not allow me to believe such rubbish and although I had no plans to marry the man, I did care about his wellbeing.

Paul had left something for me in my room the night he failed to pick me up from work. Red baby roses, a box of my favorite chocolates and a short note of love adorned my dresser. The note attached to the floral arrangement read "only you." Paul could be such a gentleman at times. Maybe I was a fool to pass him up but I was madly in love with a flame known as Scarlet Rose Laveau. I just prayed in the end that I would not get burnt too badly. If there was the slightest chance for Scarlet and I to be together, I was willing to risk it all.

I asked Scarlet if Paul had come by at all that day or night. I knew that he could not have come through the window to leave the gifts. I made sure to lock my bedroom windows whenever I left the house and they were still locked. However, Scarlet said that he must have come through another open window in the house because she had not seen Paul. It was highly unlikely that Scarlet would let Paul in the house anyhow, and Paul would not have wanted to be there without me. I decided that he must have come through another window like Scarlet had said, because there was no other explanation. All I knew was that something terrible had happened to Paul and he had no way of letting me know. In desperation I finally went back to Scarlet. I did not know where else to turn and I needed to know the truth about Paul.

Scarlet was laid half naked on the couch with nothing but a thigh length skirt exposing the red and lace panties that covered her crotch. She was listening to Etta Jones blaring from the record player. Scarlet's eyes were closed but moving beneath and letting me know that she was aware of my presence. I wanted to lie atop of her and suck on her exposed breast that fit perfectly in the palm of my hands. I stood admiring her before speaking. I lingered a bit and she allowed it because it was her way of staying in control of a situation.

She had these weird scratches on her arm and a slight cut beneath her bottom lip. "Scarlet." I said in almost a whisper, not wanting to disturb her obvious relaxed mood.

"Yes Koral." Scarlet replied without opening her eyes to acknowledge me.

"What happened to your face and arm?"

"It was an accident really. Brazil and I were playing rough is all."

Too rough don't you think? "I'm worried about Paul. This is so unlike him. Something must be wrong with him."

Scarlet sat up on the sofa with her lengthy locs embracing her like a red cape. She bit down on her bottom lip and stared at me before requesting my hands by holding out hers. I went to her and kneeled before her half bare body placing my hands over hers before allowing them to meet. I could feel the heat from Scarlet's palms; it was a sign that would almost always bring bad news. I looked to her for hope but she shook her head. I flopped down near her feet and buried my head in her uncovered lap. She caressed the back of my head as I watered her legs with my concern for Paul. I gathered myself within seconds and demanded to know what had happened to Paul.

"Scarlet just tell me what has happened, I cannot go on not knowing."

"It is not clear Koral. But I cannot feel any warmth from Pierre. He is cold and without thought wherever he is."

"But… but that sounds as if he is dead." I said pushing my body back a little to get a clear picture of Scarlet's expression.

"I'm sorry Koral. I wish I knew more. Maybe later we can try again. For now, do not trouble yourself with such things."

"Oh Paul." I cried.

Scarlet rubbed me with her hands.

"Whatever has happened could not have been avoided. Life will happen my love, we have no choice but to live it or leave it."

"I've been so bad to him. I just wish he knew that I cared."

"He knows. Now stop your weeping."

I prayed that Paul did know. I wish that I could tell him how great he had been to me and how much I appreciated him. *Lord please give me the chance to tell Paul how I feel.*

"You think maybe Brazil would be willing to help?" I asked with caution as to not downplay Scarlet's talent.

"Help with what?" She asked coldly.

I stumbled over my words and came down to my baby voice as to not upset Scarlet.

"To maybe help me file a missing persons report or to see if he is in a hospital or morgue somewhere."

"I told you he is cold. A cold body is not lying up in no hospital bed Koral Baptiste."

Scarlet was being insensitive. I knew there was no love lost between them but she loved me and should have been more understanding of my needs.

"I'm sorry Scarlet. I know that you are right but since you said that your vision was not all that clear I was just wondering…"

"Do not wonder. You can do the same thing that Brazil can do. Pick up the phone or go down to the precinct. I will not be troubling her over something no one can do anything about."

I was hoping that Scarlet would be more understanding considering the circumstances. But she was right, if I wanted to know of Paul I should do it myself. All I had to do was call around or go and file a missing persons report on Paul's behalf.

Brazil and Scarlet had become closer than ever. My worse fear was coming true. I was losing the love of my life to another. I finally understood how Paul must have felt about Scarlet and I. I do not even know how a routine trip to question a person about a suicide victim turns into a romance. They were even building a garden together with a sidewalk entrance to it. Scarlet had always been into flowers but usually only planted them around the front of the house. She told me that Brazil wanted to give her a nice gift and so they started a garden in the backyard. Scarlet had been outback earlier planting more seeds and even had plans to put a bench back there. It seemed as if Scarlet could tame the damn devil himself. If I wanted Scarlet at all, I was going to have to fight for her attention. I knew I already had her love but I wanted it all and not just a part of her. And besides, I did not see her dating anyone other than Officer Brazil Tio. Maybe she would grow tired of her soon. Scarlet was good at that, meeting new people and getting rid of them. Just some lasted longer than others but none had lasted as long as me.

I had been in Scarlet's life forever and I was determined to die that way. I knew one thing she wanted more than a new damn garden and I would make sure that she got that from me before she decided to ask Brazil. Although I knew Scarlet was smart enough to not ask a cop to help her murder someone. I was the only one she would trust with that secret. Helping Scarlet fulfill her desire would prove just how much I loved her and that would win her over for sure.

First things first, I needed to file that missing persons report on Paul. Lord help him if I found out that he skipped town without at least letting me know not to worry about him. I may not have been the best girlfriend but I did care about Paul and would never want anything bad to happen to him. He was a great guy over all. He just was not Scarlet and that was really my issue with him.

It was my day off and I wanted to go down to the police station and see if they could possibly check the morgues and hospitals for any signs of Paul. I would feel better knowing that I had made some sort of effort to clear my mind and conscience.

The minute I opened the squeaky screened door to step out onto the porch, my nostrils were filled with the smell of rain approaching. All I needed was for it to rain. I went back to fetch my umbrella and on my way out I ran right smack into Brazil. That damn woman could not stay away from Scarlet for even a day. I wanted to avoid her all together but we were standing face to face and somebody needed to speak. Brazil was about to step into my home, it would have been the polite thing for her to speak first. My Nana raised me up with good manners and so I decided to break the awkward moment with a smile and a warm hello.

"Hello Brazil, how are you?" I pretended to care.

"It's about to rain you know?"

"Yes, thank you. I have a matter that cannot wait. I am actually headed to your precinct."

"Is there anything I can help you with?" She asked curiously.

"Only if you can take a missing persons report?"

"I'm off duty right now. But if it will save you a trip I will take the report. Who is missing?"

"My boyfriend Paul." I said.

I thought about Scarlet not wanting me to bother Brazil with my issues. I wanted to say never mind but she kept right on with the questions.

"Why would you assume that he was missing?"

"It is not like him to not come see me or pick me up from work and his landlord has not heard anything from him either and all of his things are still in his room."

Brazil seemed truly concerned and she did offer to help. I was just hoping that Scarlet would not be upset about it.

"Maybe they were not worth taking. People leave all the time. I'll tell you what, write down everything that you know about him and I will check out a few things and let you know."

Perhaps Brazil Tio was not so bad after all. She was willing to help me with Paul and did not know him. Maybe I had judged her too harshly, but one thing she was wrong about was Paul. I was worth everything to him and he would not have just up and left me. Scarlet was right, he had to be hurt or, God forbid, dead. That is the only thing that would stop my yellow fellow from showing up. I would just have to pray for the best outcome and a good explanation from Paul whenever I did see him.

Now that I was not going to the precinct, I didn't know what to do with myself. I wanted to talk to Scarlet but she had company now, hell, she always had company lately. I needed some time alone with her. I decided to find things around the house to do in hopes of buying time and patience to speak with my best friend and lover. Hopefully Brazil would leave soon and I would make sure to have that information about Paul ready for her. At least something good would come out of her visiting.

I still did not know what Scarlet saw in Brazil. I was much more of a woman if she so desired to have one at the moment. Scarlet was like the wind, forever blowing in an aimless direction. And many days I just got blown off for the next victim but I was willing to wait my turn again. It would always be my turn again.

I watched Scarlet from the hallway getting dressed for one of her ceremonies. That was a part of her life that Nana had warned me to never be a part of. I was always curious about them and wanted to go despite what Nana thought. It was Scarlet that told me I was not ready to let go of my homemade beliefs. I did not understand why I could not be a Christian and still share in her world.

I had heard so many things from the locals about such things. They said that those rituals were in honor of the devil himself. Not that I believed any of that foolishness. Scarlet had taught me better. I was just afraid and spooked by it all, even the stories that Scarlet had shared over the years. I once watched her do a praise dance and I was so afraid of what I witnessed, surely there was something else there. Scarlet's voiced changed and her body jerked so violently, I thought she would fall apart but when she stopped she was all smiles. I prayed something fiercely after I returned home that night. I would not judge and I was not able to join her, but I could love her. Scarlet finally acknowledged my presence.

"Don't just stand there and stare, come talk to me for a moment, I'll be heading out soon." Scarlet said.

She was standing there admiring herself dressed in her usual ceremonial clothing. It was amazing how she could have on something so simple and reap of nothing but sex. I cleared my mind of wanting to devour her and tried to be serious. I knew that she could read my thoughts and although I was not ashamed of them, I wanted to take advantage of having her alone for a change. Brazil had left a lil earlier, but not before she stopped by my room to get the information on Paul. I had thanked Brazil and bided her a goodnight.

I set on the edge of Scarlet's twin bed directly behind her as she stared back at me from the mirror in front of her.

"I think I'm ready... no, I know I'm ready. I feel like I need to do something major to get all of this aggression from inside of me Scarlet."

"Ready for what?" She said as if she had no clue of what I spoke about. She wanted to hear me say it. I knew this woman so very well.

"For us to experience something so very deep together. I am ready for the kill Scarlet. Hell, I'm more than ready. Honestly... I would be willing to do it tonight."

Scarlet turned and batted her accusing eyes at me. "Are you now? Do you have someone in mind?"

Before I could think straight I answered and then regretted it shortly after. "Yeah, Brazil."

Out of nowhere Scarlet doubled over in laughter and I soon joined her after the fear of her actions left me.

"Sweet Koral, I have been ready for years. You have no idea what this means to me. I will make sure to show you just how much when I return tonight." Scarlet said kissing me with her wet tongue.

Scarlet left soon after we finished kissing. It was enough to send my heart racing like any other time that she paid me attention. I would make groceries and plan a meal with her favorite dessert to welcome her back home and into my arms. Brazil's time was almost up and I was planning to make sure of it. I wouldn't let anything keep me from the woman that I loved.

Chapter Fifteen
Scarlet

Nana stood there gawking at me as if I had wronged her in some sort of way. I hated when people judged me without knowing all of the details. Details are just as important as the act. You cannot crucify a woman for being the only thing she knew how to be. But I was used to her accusations and I also knew that she had followed Koral into my home. I was expecting her and had been sensing Nana the entire time.

I sat there in my old white wooden rocker next to my bedroom window staring back at her. I wanted her to know that I did not fear her and that there was nothing left of her to be frightened of. I have always wondered why people feared the dead. It was a little too late for them to do us any harm. The only damage that the deceased could bring to the living was what we would allow. Things come back to hurt us when we are not prepared, I stayed ready.

Nana just stood there with her raggedy self and attempted to spook me. The woman never did care for me. She judged me for being different and for her Koral loving me more. People did not want to understand the love between women that went past the emotional stage. We were all lesbians when connected spiritually, but who wanted to admit to that? Nana had always fussed at Koral and I about being too feely touchy when we were kids. She said that it was unnatural for girls to behave in such a way and to cut it out. Nana would threaten to switch us real good if she caught us cuddling again. I just could not comprehend why it bothered her so much. We were kids and the love between us was a natural thing.

Nana was always nice to me in front of my parents but as soon as we were alone she was warning me about this and that. I only put up with her nonsense so that Koral and I could be together. And I think that Nana understood that there was no way to break us apart without damaging Koral. She had already lost enough people in her life.

"Don't just stand there looking stupid. I did you a favor old woman, only I should have done it much sooner."

Nana seemed to hiss at me and so I hissed back. *I ain't afraid of no ghost!* I pulled my legs up in the chair and opened them to expose myself. I assumed that masturbating would send the old hag to roam in another part of the house. Nana vanished as soon as my fingers went across my protruding clit. I laughed aloud and yelled after her. "You don't have to leave so soon do you?"

Things between Brazil and I were pretty serious. I had to keep reminding myself that unlike Koral, I did not completely know this woman. Koral had been mine to do as I pleased with for many years. Brazil was new and although she was eager, there was something else inside of her that I was trying to pull to the surface. I did not like surprises and I could not deal with an unstable woman or man. Whomever I chose to spend my love on had to be a soldier in every meaning of the word. I needed her to not only be willing to die for me but kill as well. And I did not mean in a serial killer type of way. I just wanted someone willing to defend my honor and body with their own in an instant.

I absolutely knew that Brazil Tio had it in her to be the best warrior in my army. She had proved herself worthy of me by taking care of the situation with Pierre. I was just wondering if she would have been so willing to help if she knew the truth of it all.

That was something I would need to figure out somehow. I knew that she had convinced Koral that she would look into Pierre's disappearance. Brazil was clever in deciding to pretend to help Koral instead of actually filing a missing persons report. The longer that we avoided dealing with Paul's disappearance the better our chances would be of getting away with it.

Brazil was on her way over. We had plans to have dinner together. I had a romantic evening intended to show her my appreciation for everything that she had done and also to get to know even more about her. Koral working late nights always left my evenings free to do as I pleased. Not that her being home would stop me from being free. It made it easier when her possessive and jealous spirit was not around and at times it made the sex with Brazil a whole lot better. Brazil was more vocal during sex when Koral was not at home.

Koral would work my body overtime trying to prove how much better she was than Brazil when we had sex. Not that Koral ever claimed to be a better lover. I knew it from the difference in our sex. It was more aggressive and filled with motives. I had to figure out how to deal with it all before Brazil caught on that Koral and I were best friends that made love as well.

I stood over the stove adding a dash of olive oil to the water for the spaghetti noodles when a set of arms reached around my waist to embrace me. I turned to greet the woman that smelled of sweet coconut.

"The door was opened. Is that safe this time of night?" Brazil asked.

I rolled my eyes. "I could leave a welcome mat out and no one would dare enter without permission. This has always been a safe haven."

"Is that why you stay?"

"No. I have no reason to leave. This is my home… where I belong."

"And if I wanted you to go away with me?" Brazil said while holding onto my eyes with hers.

How could I answer that honestly without offending her so early in the evening.

"Where would we go?"
"Anywhere that you so desired."
"Then, I desire to be here." I said with a wicked smile and a kiss to end the dreadful conversation.

No way was I leaving the Big Easy unless it was against my will. I planned to die right here and be cremated and sprinkled out down by the bayou.

"What's for dinner?" Brazil asked looking over my shoulder.
"Spaghetti. It is about time I make our thing official."
"Make what official?"

I laughed to make a joke out of a serious statement. Although I had Brazil eating out the palm of my hands, there was nothing wrong with assuring that things stayed that way. A little blood would not hurt her and I am sure she would not even notice the difference.

"Dinner is almost ready. Why don't you go put on some music and open the wine for us?" I said shooing her out of the kitchen so that I could fix plates.

I had a special sauce just for her and I did not need her questioning why there were two different sauces. It was something that I kept on hand for those that I wanted around for a lifetime.

We ate dinner in the dining room. I hardly ever used that area except for special occasions and when my parents visited. As with the rest of the house, everything was exactly as Momma Laveau had left it. I had no reason to replace good furniture. The oversized mahogany table and china cabinet would outlive me. I kept it polished and set up with the same dishes that my father had given to my mother for their anniversary years ago.

I looked over at Brazil enjoying her bloody spaghetti and smiled at her. "Good?"

"The best ever," She replied in her sexy raspy voice.

She was the perfect combination of man and woman and with her you did not have to decide, you got the best of both in one. I wondered for a moment if I could truly be happy with just one person. Could Brazil Tio complete me? Then I thought about Koral and how her whole life was centered on me. Something would have to change and that something would have to be sooner than later. I drained the rest of the wine from my glass and held it out for my little androgen to fill it back up. Not that she was small, just new in my life. Brazil was very well built with strong arms and legs. And I do believe that many men were and would be intimidated by her presence.

I stared Brazil down while licking the wine from my lips to make suggestions for dessert other than the jelly cake that sat before her. Just as she was about to respond, there was a knock on the door. I knew that it was not Koral because she was still on the clock at work and she also had keys to a door that was not locked. I excused myself from the table to find out who had come without prior notice or invite.

"I shall return shortly."

"Do hurry. I miss you already." Brazil teased.

My mysterious visitor was standing in the view from the screened door looking sideways at something when I approached the door. I spotted his yellow work vehicle before I even saw his face and recognized who it was. I opened the door to step out of the house to speak with him. *Why the hell do you assume that it was okay to just stop by.*

"Philly?"

Philly embraced me as if it was a routine thing and handed me a bottle of wine. He looked a little confused when I did not invite him in and laughed a nervous laugh.

"Can I come in?" He asked shaking his head.

I was still amazed at his audacity to show up uninvited. "This is not okay with me."

I backed away from him while peering through the screen of the door to make sure that Brazil was not watching.

"I'm sorry Scarlet."

"You should have called Philly."

"I know, I lost your number and got desperate. I wanted to see you again, is that a crime?"

"Not a crime, but not okay."

Philly placed his hands on his hips and gave me this stupid ass look.

"Why not? Shit it is cold out here."

"I have company Philly."

"Oh I see. You fucking another dude in my circle?"

I laughed a little in remembrance of Philly and I making out in the ceremonial room. I placed my fingers on his lips to quiet him and allowed them to linger at the ring that hugged his bottom lip. I wanted to snatch it out as a warning and to watch him bleed but I did not need the scene that would take place after. I had to get rid of him before Brazil showed up at the door.

"Look my tattooed one nighter, get over yourself and comeback tomorrow during the day if you still want to see me. I have my girlfriend over at the moment."

"You dyking tonight?"

"Is that even a word Philly? Now go please before I change my mind."

Philly left as I suggested. I stood there watching the sexy tattooed white boy enter his cab and pull away before returning to Brazil.

I walked back into the house and closed the front door behind me this time. I needed privacy for what I had premeditated for after dinner. Brazil sat enjoying a glass of wine when I entered the dining room. Her plate was clean and she appeared to be satisfied but still I offered more.

"Would you like more?" I asked.

I stood behind her and ran my hands down the cropped ponytail that she sported. Her hair was always pulled back but not in a bun this time.

"No. I am full, but thank you kindly."

"Dessert?"

"Not now Scarlet. Who was that at the door?" She asked to my surprise.

Was Brazil being possessive already or just nosey?

"An old friend." I smirked.

"An old boyfriend? Because I heard him ask to come in and the way he just stopped over has me wondering? And here I thought that you were a lesbian."

"I never claimed to be a fucking lesbo Brazil. I am Scarlet and damn proud of it."

"Who is Scarlet? Some bisexual chick that I have to worry about having men around in fear that she might want dick the next moment?"

Brazil had some fucking nerve. I started to call her ass out. She had been pretending to be straight and was a closeted lesbian before hooking up with me.

"You sound fucking ridiculous. Bisexuality is about freedom, not fucking a different sex every other night."

"Really now?"

"How fucking rude and disrespectful is that? Besides I do not believe in titles. I am not bisexual, I'm just me. And my interest is right here in front of me."

The conversation with Brazil was going wrong quickly and she was pissing me off with her want-to-be gold-star-lesbian ass. One thing I refused to deal with was closed minded folks. I did not want Brazil pushing off her standards of living on me. I hope she understood that trust was the only way that we could make it as anything. Life was truly too short to spend time fighting over shit that could not be controlled.

"Scarlet, I'm sorry. I had no right to come at you like that. Not like we made it official."

"Is that what you want?"

"Of course, but only when you are ready… no pressure from me baby."

I was so happy that it did not take much time for Brazil to come to her senses. I cut her a big slice of Jelly cake and fed her only a corner of it from my fingertips before I became dessert on my own dining room table. Brazil picked me up and placed me on the table before sitting back down in her chair. She helped herself to a mouthful of my pussy. I wrapped my legs around her neck and rode her face as if it was one of those mechanical bulls down at the Rodeo Club.

Folks continued to show up unannounced, only this time the folks were my parents. They called to tell me that they would be visiting me for a few days before heading to Texas to visit friends. As much as I loved my parents, having more than a half a day notice would have been more than kind.

I knew that they were really coming because I had refused the many invitations to visit them as of late. I had a lot going on in my life and I did not have time to go all the way down to Florida for a visit at that time. I knew that this was all Daddy Laveau's doing. My momma was more considerate than that. My daddy enjoyed popping up on me as if he wanted to catch me doing something wrong. I loved them both dearly but wanted their visit to be short and quick. I should have just went and visited for a few days like they had requested instead of having them here. Oh well, I would have to make the best of it. *Fuck.*

We were all sitting in the living room. Mama Laveau still referred to it as a parlor. I honestly thought that my mother lived in a fantasy world mentally. It was easier for her to pretend that her reality was a lot more than what she could afford. Momma gave up a lot of money when she married my daddy.

My grandpa Joseph Ogden, whom I have never met, had been well off. He owned more than a few funeral homes in Louisiana. Momma said he cut her off from a steady and generous monthly allowance. Grandpa Joseph also wrote her out of his will and told Momma Laveau that there was never a reason to return home. He said there would be nothing there for her ever again.

I imagine that Grandpa Joseph had to love my momma just as much as my daddy did at one point. It was hard to not love Momma Laveau. There was something magnetizing about her. Everyone that met her fell in love with her.

Koral and I sat on the floor near the couch that my parents were sitting on. It was like old times when Momma and Daddy Laveau told us stories from their past and from their parents' past. It was always a time to treasure. We were laughing it up over a story that my daddy was sharing with us when we were all startled by banging on the front door. We had so many visitors from the neighborhood coming over to see my folks. We were prepared for company but this knock was not the friendly kind.

Daddy Laveau looked to me for answers as if they were lying in my lap. He got to his feet and headed to the door with the rest of us watching after him. Daddy swung the door open as if he was prepared to ward off any trouble that may have come a knocking.

We could clearly hear the police asking for Koral and then my father telling them to come in and speak to her. Daddy held the door opened for the police and led them into the living area where Koral and I were both standing now.

"Koral Baptiste?" Asked the older white and wrinkly cop.

The other cop just stood silent writing in his day book like most did. I always wondered why a second cop was needed to do nothing.

"Yes, I'm Koral Baptiste." She said all worried.

"Are you familiar with a Pierre DePaul?"

Koral's concerned eyes went from one cop to the other and back again.

"Why yes, he is my boyfriend. Well... supposedly."

"Supposedly? Care to explain?"

"Well he went missing weeks ago and I have not heard anything from him. The man proposed to me and then just up and disappeared without a reason or word."

"When was the last time you spoke with Mr. DePaul?"

Koral scratched her head.

"Maybe three weeks ago now. We went for a picnic in City Park and then he brought me home."

"And that is the last that you saw Mr. DePaul?" The cop continued.

Koral started to tear and looked to me for help. I decided that it was best not to intrude at that moment.

"Well yes, other than him leaving flowers and a gift here while I was at work, that is the last I heard from him. Is he in some kind of trouble?"

I hoped that Koral would have failed to mention the flowers. It placed Pierre in my home the night he disappeared. Hopefully the cops would not think much of it since he was Koral's boyfriend and all.

"That is what we are trying to find out ma'am. His car was found abandoned at an old warehouse. And if he left town, he left in a hurry because he did not take any of his belongings."

The tears were flowing now. "Abandoned? Paul would never do that, he loved that car."

"Paul?"

"Yes, Pierre DePaul. Paul for short."

"I see. Did you say that he left gifts here for you? Did someone else here see him after you?"

"Yes, he climbed through my bedroom window to leave them as he usually did. No one has seen him." Koral said a little embarrassed.

Daddy Laveau raised his eyebrows. He looked to me as if I was responsible for Koral allowing Pierre to climb into her bedroom.

"Well, Ms. Baptiste, if you happen to hear from or of Mr. DePaul, please give us a call." The old fellow said while handing Koral a card with a name and number on it.

The cops left seemingly satisfied. It was Daddy Laveau that still had questions after we were all alone again. He questioned Koral again, trying to get her to remember anything that she may have forgot. I wished daddy would just leave it alone.

I wondered what Brazil was doing, I truly missed her. I had asked her to give me a few days alone with my parents and I would let her know when they were gone. I seriously thought about sneaking her in through my own bedroom window. She had been really understanding about it not being the right time to meet the folks.

Daddy Laveau just did not want to understand the whole lesbian thing. He thought my love for women was just a sexual defiance since I still dated men. Daddy Laveau would always compare it to a ménage trios that he had before meeting my momma. I did not have the heart nor the desire to continue trying to convince him that there was no difference in men and women to me.

After Daddy Laveau grilled Koral again, she told him how she had asked my friend Brazil to look into Paul's disappearance. My Daddy kept eyeing me sideways. I wanted to just snap on him but did not want to upset Momma Laveau. She was already disturbed by the situation. Momma sat there shaking her legs uncontrollably. Daddy placed his hand on her lap to help calm her a bit.

"Scarlet, are you absolutely sure that you did not hear anything the night that Paul was here? I know how you sense things and all." Daddy accused without bluntly blaming.

"I do not think I was home daddy. I was out with my friend Brazil part of the night and then we came back here together and she was with me for the rest of that night."

Koral excused herself from the room, obviously upset over Pierre. My mother went after her and my daddy continued to harass me.

"Scarlet, has your mother ever told you about the rumor surrounding your grandfather and his success in the funeral business?"

"No, she never has. I'm sure you will enlighten me."

"You are a lot like your grandpa Joseph in many ways. Joseph and his mother are the reasons for this special gift that you and your mother have. It has been in your family history for a long time. Some used it for good and others did not."

I am not about to sit through this bullshit.

"Why are you telling me this now? I should be comforting Koral."

Daddy waved his hand and continued to talk. "Your momma will take care of Koral for now. As I was saying, Joseph was a poor kid who was determined to be rich by all means necessary."

"I could care less about money. So we do not have that in common." I said and rolled my eyes at my daddy's intentions.

Daddy Laveau told me that Grandpa Joseph started out with one funeral parlor in a place where people lived a long time and accidents were rare. Daddy said that Grandpa Joseph felt like he would fail. That is when his funeral business picked up out of the blue and one accident happened after another. So many people were dying in Grandpa's part of town as well as surrounding areas. It was rumored that Joseph Ogden was killing his own clients to make his business a triumph. People also said that he murdered anyone that found out about it or got in his way of success.

"I can't imagine any of that nonsense is true?"

"Can't you?"

"Whatever do you mean daddy?" I said with a sweet smile and a slight air of arrogance.

I was a little intrigued by the story but sick of the accusations that Daddy Laveau made towards me. My parents would be leaving the next day and I could hardly wait to get my daddy out of my hair.

I thought about how my own Grandpa had been a serial killer. I knew that my desires did not fall far from the family tree. I always wondered if my momma was as good as she claimed to be or if she had some hidden and terrifying secret. I guess I was right about both. My momma a goody-two-shoes and her daddy was a mass murderer. I actually wish I could have known the bastard but he wanted nothing to do with my half black ass.

Chapter Sixteen
Koral

The Laveau's visit reminded me just how much I missed Nana. I almost wanted them to stay. It was nice having parents around and they treated me as if I was a child of their own. I knew that Scarlet did not want them to stay, but it would be good to have them at least closer so that we could visit more. I enjoyed everything about the Laveau's and Scarlet was so blessed to have such wonderful parents that were always there for her.

Paul's mysterious disappearance had me so worried and nervous that I had to call out from work. I wanted to look for him myself to see if I could get some answers. I visited the places Paul frequented to see if he had been there, but he had not. I also asked his landlord if it would be okay to look around his room for any clues. He said he did not mind on the count of him having to pack Paul's room up soon for nonpayment. The landlord told me to take what I wanted as well because Paul was not coming back. He spoke as if Paul was already dead or something. I hated when people assumed the worst all the time.

Paul's room was as if he was just out and would be back. He had things in there that I knew he would never leave behind. There were his family albums and a record collection that he insisted were heirlooms. His clothing was half packed and half still hanging. It would be an awful shame if Paul spent his life time trying to get away from New Orleans just to die in it. How fair would that be?

I cried as I gathered a few of his things that would matter to him when and if he returned. I paid the Landlord to store the rest of Paul's things in his basement for the time being. He did not charge me much on the count of him liking Paul and all. Paul did annoy me at times but he did treat me like a queen and only wanted the best for me. I just really wanted a chance to tell him just what it had all meant to me. *Lord is that asking too much?*

I took the bus home because I was in no rush to get there. Maybe I should have gone to work. I just did not want to be there crying my eyes out like some mad woman. I sat there on the bus with my legs crossed looking out of the window at nothing but my last moments with Paul. I wished like hell that I could go back to that day in City Park and just enjoy it. I could not control my tears at that point and people started to stare. I dug in my purse for a tissue but was all out and so I turned my head further toward the window and used the collar of my black and white striped dress to wipe first my tears and then my runny nose.

The bus slowly approached my stop. I stood to pull the line in order to let the driver know that I would be exiting at the next bus stop. I could see Scarlet's sky blue house trimmed in what seemed like perfect pink sitting in the midst of the other homes. It was as if her home was the only house on the block and definitely the one with a story. I lost sight of the place I called home only for a moment as I stepped down from the side exit of the bus onto the street. I felt a bit dizzy and almost lost my balance. I realized that my body was in need of some food in it. Being worried over Paul left no room for an appetite.

I walked towards that house with so many emotions tumbling inside of me. I found myself in deep need and want of my Nana. I was so worried about Paul and not knowing his fate drove me insane. And then there was dear Scarlet. Would I lose Scarlet as well? Could I lose Scarlet and still survive at all. I felt as if she was all that I had that reminded me that I belonged somewhere and with somebody. I needed her to myself more than ever now. I just hoped and prayed that she would not fail me.

I rushed inside the house hoping to find Scarlet there waiting for me but she was nowhere to be found. I went to her room to lie in her bed to feel close to her. I just wanted to smell her if I could not touch her at that moment. I lay in her bed holding on to Ruben. Ruben was a stuffed animal that was just as old as Scarlet and me. How I wished at that moment that we were girls with no worries again. Life was truly a big deal when you had to face reality.

I found myself angered over wondering if Scarlet was with Brazil. I twisted and turned Paul's ring on my finger. I started daydreaming about Scarlet proposing to me in front of Brazil. Then the ring slipped and fell from my bony fingers to the floor and rolled beneath Scarlet's bed. I started to leave it there, because what did it matter now? I could not even find Paul to give it back if I wanted to and everybody else seemed to think of him as dead already.

I got down from the bed and crawled beneath it to retrieve the ring. I stayed in the position for a while tracing the ring and remembered how Scarlet and I hid under this very bed. We gave each other promise rings that we got from one of those toy machines in the grocery store. Scarlet had truly been the love of my life for all of my life. Our love had always been far deeper than innocent could hold and I guess that is what Nana feared. I knew that I always had looked to Scarlet as not just love but a lover and a safe haven at a very early age.

Just as I was about to pull my body from beneath the bed, something familiar caught my eye. It was part of Paul's keychain slightly hidden by a shoe box. Paul had this green, gold and purple keychain that said, "I've found the love of my life in New Orleans." It was only a part of a broken keychain that I found but I was quite certain that it was Paul's. I recalled seeing it hanging from his keychain the day that he dropped me off after our picnic. My head started to spin and I wondered what it all meant and why would anything of Paul's be beneath Scarlet's bed. The possibilities of a meaning frightened me a bit. I got from under Scarlet's bed quickly and headed to my room to put the piece of keychain in a safe place. I needed time to think and find a way to approach Scarlet about it without her thinking that I was accusing her of anything. I did not want Scarlet to think that I had been snooping about her room when it was not the truth.

I woke later that evening to voices. Once again, Brazil was over and she and Scarlet were making out rather loudly with no consideration for my feelings or comfort. I really needed to speak with Scarlet alone and it was becoming damn near impossible to do so with Brazil in the picture. I started to fear that she might just up and move in without notice and surely then I would lose Scarlet forever. I was not willing to let that happen. I decided at that moment to take control of things for once and for all. I would have to use what I had in order to get Scarlet back. I had no plans on losing everything to some cop that had only been in our lives for a few months.

I leaped from bed and grabbed the piece of keychain that belonged to Paul and went storming towards Scarlet's door. Did she just up and forget the love that we had made in that very bed every night that her parents had been here. I would no longer let

Scarlet think that it was cool to just love on me when she felt like it. I would help her come to her senses and realize that we were meant to be together forever. I pounded on Scarlet's door until Brazil decided to answer, although I was expecting Scarlet to. I knew at that point the situation with Brazil was getting way to serious. Never had I known Scarlet to let someone be in control of her space.

"Yes?" Brazil said all annoyed.

She had opened the door only halfway as if I were a stranger. I could see her naked ass from the light that spilled down the hall from my bedroom.

"I need to see Scarlet." I demanded without any further explanation.

"Scarlet is tied up right now." Brazil chuckled with Scarlet joining in from the background.

"Well just you tell her that this cannot wait and I will be waiting for her in my room." I said loud enough for Scarlet to hear and turned to leave.

I sat on the edge of my bed trying to decide if I was angry or jealous. Maybe I was both and rightfully so. Within minutes Scarlet was at my door obviously irritated at my request but curious at my odd behavior.

"Koral, what's gotten into you? Are you ill or something?"

"No, I need to speak with you in private and I need it to be now!"

"Okay… I'm here. Do you want me to close the door or something?" Scarlet asked rolling her eyes and looking behind her.

"No, I want you to ask Brazil to leave so that we can talk about Paul."

"Dammit Koral, can't it wait til the morning? And why aren't you at work anyhow?"

"I called out." I said looking down.

I almost lost the courage to do what I set out to do. But the smell of sex coming from Scarlet renewed my strength to go through with it. I stood and approached Scarlet.

"What is it Koral, just spill it please." Scarlet insisted.

"I said I need for you to ask Brazil to leave now." I repeated while showing her Paul's keychain.

"What is that?"

"Used to be a part of Paul's keychain." I responded sarcastically.

"What does that have to do with me?" She asked angrily.

"I don't know, you tell me?"

"Tell you what?" Scarlet said lowering her voice to a whisper.

"Why I found this under your bed today, when it was on Paul's keychain last I saw him?"

Scarlet stared as if she expected me to back down.

"Let me ask Brazil to leave, because you have obviously lost your fucking mind." Scarlet said storming out of my room and down the hall.

I wished at that moment that I could have been the fly on the wall when she asked Brazil to leave in the middle of what sounded like great sex. I knew in that moment that I was willing to do anything and everything it took to get Brazil out of our lives for good.

The minute I heard Brazil's car leave and the house door slam shut I knew that Scarlet was mad with rage. She was back at the entry of my bedroom door breathing like an angry dragon in need of destroying her prey. Scarlet was still beautiful even in anger. Her face was full of as much fire as her hair. I wanted to feel the heat that was coming from her presence inside of me.

"Now explain yourself Koral!" Scarlet demanded.

"No! You explain why Paul's key chain would be beneath your bed?" I demanded back.

"I cannot believe for a minute that you would think that I had anything to do with Pierre's death. I did not like him but I did not kill him either Koral."

I looked my best friend up and down. "Who said anything about Paul being dead?" I questioned.

"I did... remember with the reading? Do not sit here and use a gift that has helped you many times against me now." Scarlet replied coming to sit with and comfort me.

I fell apart right in her arms. I could not hold up to all the weight that was on my shoulders. I did not want to push Scarlet away. I needed her like never before.

"Scarlet I miss my Nana so much and I miss you as well."

"We are both here Koral."

"Both?" I said sitting up and wiping my eyes.

"Yes, I will never leave you and Nana is sitting on the other side of you wishing that you could sense her presence."

"Is she saying anything? Tell her that I'm sorry that I was not there when she needed me the most. Tell her Scarlet, tell her please."

"Koral calm down a bit now. Nana is not going anywhere and she can hear you just fine."

"I'm sorry Scarlet."

"Nana says to stop all of this nonsense and for us to continue looking out for each other. She said that she was wrong about me and that she is happy that I took you in."

Scarlet reached over to soothe the space opposite of me and spoke with Nana. She promised to care for me and told Nana not to worry that everything would be okay soon. Scarlet then insisted that we share a warm bath and leftover dinner from the night before.

We sat in the tub opposite each other without words at first. Then Scarlet told me how much she loved and cared about my wellbeing. She said that we had to be strong and work through our obstacles. Later at the dinner table she promised that everything would make sense to me soon.

I remember falling asleep in Scarlet's arms. The place I wanted to be the most, only to wake up to being all alone in my bed and to the sounds of a strange and awkward cry coming from the hall. I went to open my bedroom door only to find darkness and there was no light anywhere and the crying had ceased at my presence.

I went to Scarlet's room to see if she was okay. She was fast asleep in bed. I went back to my room insisting that it was a bad dream or maybe a sound from outside. Once I was back in bed I heard the crying again and it escalated. I leaped from bed again and swung open my bedroom door. I saw what seemed like a long figure walking down the hall in a long black robe that disappeared around the corner. I screamed for Scarlet and she came rushing out of her bedroom.

"What is it Koral?"

"I heard this crying and there is someone or something in this house. I saw it just turn the corner into the living room."

Scarlet walked me through the house turning on lights to prove that nothing was there. She said the mind will confuse you when sleepy. I had been having trouble getting to sleep.

Scarlet made me a warm cup of milk and gave me one of her homemade potions for relaxing and then rocked me back to sleep. I saw and heard weird shit all night but I was too drugged to get up again. I felt sort of safe with Scarlet behind me asleep. I just wished that she could hear and see what I was experiencing. I was not making this stuff up. That thing in the black robe sat across from us in the middle of the floor with its back turned just a weeping. I would fall in and out of sleep just to witness it all over again.

I arrived at work a little late after calling out three days straight. My boss was threatening to fire me and I could not afford to lose my income. Things were getting really weird at the house. I knew that Scarlet attracted ghost and I had experienced some supernatural shit with her before but never had spirits or whatever they were bothered me in such a way. I was still hearing the weeping which kept me half up most nights. Scarlet had been generous enough to give me sleeping aids to try and help me sleep. She also promised to get to the bottom of what was going on.

Scarlet said that more than likely it was a warning against something that I was doing concerning her. She told me the spirits in the house were there to protect her and would do so at all cost. Scarlet had given up offerings for peace but it did not work. Maybe it would have to come from me as Scarlet suggested. She gave me candles to burn and also offerings to leave. I hoped and prayed that whatever I had stirred up by trying to blackmail Scarlet would just go away. I loved Scarlet and would not go against her for just any reason. I just wanted to be with her, not hurt her at all.

I walked into the back of the restaurant clocked in and then grabbed my apron to put around my waist. My boss started complaining about me being late and slapped a warning slip in my hand to sign. I signed the paper without argument because I knew he needed people he could count on just like any other job would need.

Gray pulled me to the side on the first break we got. He was genuinely concerned and noted how tired and worn down I appeared.

"What's gon' on with you Koral?"
"Paul is missing and I have been sort of ill."
"Missing? What ails you?"

I told Gray almost everything, even about finding a piece of Paul's keychain. I did not tell the truth about where I found it. I refused to implicate Scarlet in any type of way. Gray must have read between the lines because the only advice he gave me was to leave Scarlet's house and her world for good.

Gray had told me before that he knew of Scarlet and the knowing was not good. I had asked him to keep any and all gossip about my best friend to himself. He assured me that gossip would often change from person to person but the truth stayed the same. Out of respect he agreed to not speak ill of Scarlet. Scarlet was hardly ever our topic until that day. Gray still kept his word about not bad talking her. He had only advised me to leave her home.

All I could think about was what kind of life I would have without Scarlet when she was my life. She really had not done anything against me. I had to get to the bottom of the keychain mystery. One thing for sure, Scarlet was not being totally honest about not seeing Paul the night he left me stranded at work. Maybe she threatened him and made him leave town, she never did want him for me. But I rather her be honest than to allow me to worry.

Chapter Seventeen
Scarlet

Koral was becoming a major issue. I needed to make absolutely certain that she would not talk to anyone about finding Pierre's keychain beneath my bed. I am not sure how I would ever be able to explain that. Especially when Koral is claiming that he had that very keychain the day before he disappeared. I had already started shaking things up a bit but I needed to do more. It was time to take Koral up on her offer. If we murdered someone together, she would have to stay quiet for life. I just had to figure out how and who.

Brazil could never know about Koral and I murdering someone. We would have to pull it off on our own. I thought about Philly again, but he never did show back up to my place again. Maybe his ego was bruised. I would have to try and call him and see if he wanted to party with Koral and I. Or better yet, we could just do a random person and just make certain that we covered our path. *Decisions, decisions.*

There comes a time in your life when mistakes are not allowed based on the path you have chosen to walk. I walked breathless in search of anything falling out of place after Pierre's death. I was in need of something higher than myself, a spiritual guide to lead me straight to safety. I realized that my actions were the only things standing between me staying free and prison. There was no way that I could ever survive behind bars. I was born with wings and my purpose in life was to prove that some people had supernatural abilities. The mind was the place that I aimed to control within people. It was the only real insurance one had when putting your trust in another's actions. The time had come to move things into a space that could not be undone.

∞

Koral and I were posted up in a booth down at the local jazz club. I had invited her out for drinks on her day off. It had been awhile since the two of us were able to really spend some quality time alone since Brazil entered my life. I was beginning to feel a little guilty about Koral feeling abandoned and all. I knew that part of Koral's suspicion about Pierre's death was due to having too much time on her hands. I had to figure out a way to keep her busier and also make sure not to neglect Brazil.

Koral appeared to glow. She sat across from me smiling and mouthing something that I could not hear. Although the band was rather loud, my attention being on something else was what kept me from tuning in to the reason behind Koral's happiness.

"Scarlet are you here?" Koral teased.

I smiled at my only real and true friend in remembrance of better times. "I'm sorry Koral."

"Are you enjoying yourself?" She asked looking all radiant with her gorgeous brown sugar boobs spilling over the top of her low cut orange blouse. She had been so miserable lately. It was good to see her enjoying life for the moment.

"Yes, I am." I said taking a shot of tequila followed by a chug of the Corona beer that we had ordered.

"I have always admired how you handle you liquor so well my lady." Koral teased.

We both laughed followed by Koral taking the next shot and drink. In the middle of our joy, some mutt approached the table and offered to buy the next round of drinks. We accepted and asked him to join us. He was not handsome at all but rather sexy and clean cut. The goatee benefitted him in many ways. It probably masked more undesirable features. His eyes were damn near closed and way too small. I did not trust anyone with small eyes. Small eyed people had a lot unseen. I decided not to focus so much on what I did not like about him. He was perfect for murder, hell anyone would have been at that point.

"What are you two beauties getting into after you leave here?" He asked.

"Trouble." I responded and Koral laughed.

"I'm Blue. And you are?" He asked looking from me to Koral and back again.

"Red and Black. I responded, not giving Koral a chance to fuck up by giving our real names.

She sat there smirking while wiping away beer from her chin that had escaped her mouth from laughing out loud at the names.

"Red and Black huh?"

"Yeah, that's right." Koral said while ordering another round of shots from the approaching waiter.

"Well I have a room at the Inn on the corner." Blue advised.

"I see. We were in the middle of discussing a private matter. Why don't you give us a minute to finish up here and we will meet you there?"

"For certain." He replied while pulling enough money from his billfold to clear the tab and a nice tip.

Blue winked at us both while exposing the stack of bills in his wallet. I guess he expected to pay for the pussy that night. I smiled at the foolish man and punched Koral beneath the table to do the same.

"My room number is 212. What would you ladies like to drink?"

"Sazerac?" I asked Koral as she shook her head yes.

"See you in about thirty minutes?" Blue asked.

"Twenty will do." I said watching him disappear from sight.

I looked to Koral and told her that there was no better time than now to go through with our plan. We had a random guy who was just right around the corner waiting to be killed. I explained to her how she would distract him while I put something in his drink. And once we had him under our control we could decide how to finish him off. I suggested smothering the poor guy. It was a technique that I knew had been successful more than once and he would not be able to put up a fight.

I could hear Koral's heartbeat over the music and all of a sudden she looked as if she had seen a ghost already. I did not know if she was sick or just nervous about the whole ordeal. I told her not to think so much about it. Murder was easier done than said. I got up from the table.

"Let's go Koral."

"Right behind you." She said downing the rest of her Corona.

We walked out into the night and headed left to the Inn. There were many people on the street. Many of whom were trying to get our attention for one reason or another. I told Koral not to stop and talk, to just keep going. We did not need to stop and talk long enough for anyone to remember us and if they did, we would be our own alibis. Enough people knew of me in that town. It was one of the reasons that I decided to hide my red hair beneath a beanie cap that night as to not stand out as much.

We arrived at Blue's room and right before I was about to knock Koral spoke up.

"I can't do this."
"You can't or you won't?" I said in a low tone.
"I do not feel so well Scarlet."

Just then Blue's door opened and he stood smiling before looking confused at us just standing there.

"Are you sure?" I said to Koral.
"Very." She said and ran out of the hotel.
"I am sorry. She is not feeling so well and I should see her home. Maybe next time?"
"You can't stay without her?"
"No. But I have your room number and the hotel name. Should I call and reschedule?"
"Okay." Blue said looking as if someone had died. Not knowing he would have been dead within hours. It was his lucky night and one of my worst.

I smiled and turned away in all of my anger from Koral. This was the second time that she had pulled this shit on me. To make matters worse, it was her suggestion to go through with it this time. I did not believe for one moment that she was sick. She was full of shit, is what she was and I had no time for fucking games or to be made a fool of. *Bitch.*

"I'm sorry Scarlet." She repeatedly said as I used the phone booth to call for a cab. I wanted to leave the stupid bitch right on the curb. This was a waste of my time when I could have been with Brazil. She would think twice before pulling that shit again.

We rode home in silence. I was too angry to speak to her in front of the strange cabbie. But I had plans to say plenty once we reached home. There was no way that Koral was going to get away with toying with me.

∞

I jumped from the cab, leaving Koral to pay for the tab. I could not reach the front door fast enough. As quick as I unlocked it to let myself in, I slammed it shut behind me and locked it back. *Let her use her own damn key to get in.*

Koral fumbled with the door before walking in. She stormed past me standing at the entrance of the hall that led to her room. I laughed a bit wickedly as she flew down the hallway.

I went to the phone that we kept on a sofa table in the hallway between our rooms and called Brazil up. I would not waste an entire night without at least enjoying some part of it. Brazil answered on the second ring.

"Hello." She sort of sung in a raspy tone.
"Hi babe, want to come over and keep me company?"
"I thought you and Koral were hanging out. No?"
"Koral took ill and now I'm bored and all alone. And my body is aching for you." I whined loud enough for Koral to hear.

I knew that she was burning up with jealousy listening to me speak with Brazil. She should have thought about her actions that night. She could have had me all to herself. *Dumbass broad.* I hung up with Brazil and headed to the kitchen for a drink after she promised to be over soon. When I turned around Koral was approaching, she was angry and annoyed.

"Why are you so angry with me? There will be other times you know?"

"No I do not know that!" I shouted at her. "I'm not going to keep setting up shit for you to just find a stupid ass reason not to do it you know! As a matter of fact, just fucking forget it!" I said with a wave of my hand.

I walked past Koral as if she were not standing before me and tried to ignore her by going to my room.

I was certain that closing my bedroom door would end any confrontation that I felt stirring. To my surprise, the door to my bedroom flung open and Koral approached me. Something had changed about her. She had never had the guts to disrespect my space before in such a way. I knew at that moment she had lost her fucking mind and any respect that she had for me. It was very important that I took control of the situation and reminded Koral who I had been and who I still was.

Before she could get another word out her mouth I rushed over and slapped her as hard as I could. She fell back into the armoire dresser and held her face while looking to me in shock. Koral was so appealing at the moment, tears started falling from her eyes and I could not hide my pleasure in her pain. She ran from my room and into hers. I did not want to push her too far but I needed my respect back. I had given Koral access to my entire home. My room was mine, especially when I had purposely closed the door to shut her out.

I waited a few minutes before I approached her door and knocked softly. I wanted to show her the respect that she had not shown me. At first I heard only music and then her whimpering softly.

Playing music was a way that Koral drowned out whatever she did not want you to hear. She did it when Pierre used to sneak in the house as well. Some zydeco music was playing and my knocks went unanswered. I knocked a little louder and called out her name.

"Koral, Koral can I come in please."

"No, go away."

"I want to apologize for hurting you. Please let me come in."

"The door is opened Scarlet and besides it is your house."

I opened the door and crawled onto the bed to sit behind Koral. Her back was facing me and she was looking out of the window at nothing but the dark. I slid up behind her, placing Koral's body between my legs and wrapped my arms around her. I laid my head on the back of hers. Koral's curls felt so soft against my face and they smelled as if she washed them in wild strawberries. I stayed in that position for a moment inhaling her scent.

"I'm so sorry Koral. I never meant to make you cry." I said rubbing my face in her hair and squeezing her tighter.

Koral rubbed my hands to let me know that it was okay. There were no words between us, just silent acknowledgement. We stayed in that position until the rain started coming down outside and into Koral's windows. The wind was blowing like crazy and the rain was fierce. We jumped to our feet to close Koral's windows and then raced around the house to close the others.

The rain came with thunder and lightning. I grabbed an umbrella and opened the front door when I heard Brazil's car enter the drive way. I met her at the car to save her from getting soaked. She seemed grateful as we huddled under the umbrella together and made it back inside without getting too wet. As soon as we stepped into the house the lightning came with a vengeance. We all scattered around the house to unplug everything and to turn out all the lights. We did not mind the rain and thunder at all, it was the violent lightning that frightened us to stay still. Koral and I knew of many in our hood that had been struck by lightning and were never the same again.

I remember when Koral's great-aunt Frances was visiting from Maryland. She was sitting out back trying to finish up a piece of watermelon with a fork. We warned her to come in from the back porch and into the kitchen to finish her fruit but she was stubborn as a mule. Aunt Frances shooed us away and said that a lil rain never hurt anyone. And as soon as she put that fork back into her mouth the lightning struck her down into a seizure. She seemed to roll from the back steps down into Nana's yard like a huge beach ball. Her body was so big that it covered half the damn garden.

I think I was the only one that noticed how Nana seemed to be more concerned about her garden than her sister Frances. Nana cried something awful. But as she helped Aunt Frances, she kept a sick eye on her plants that had been trampled upon. I stood there laughing remembering the scene like it was yesterday.

Brazil and Koral came back to the living room wondering what was so funny. After I reminded Koral and told Brazil, we were all laughing. Koral said, "I bet Aunt Frances never did pick up another fork when it stormed." We all laughed until we cried. I realized that it was the first time that all of us had shared the same space.

The rain and lightning lingered. We soon became bored just sitting there talking about old times. I did not want to be rude and just up and leave Koral, but it was a great time to make out with Brazil. I made myself focus on something other than getting wet and decided that we were going to conjure up spirits using the Ouija board.

"Let's play with the Ouija board." I said jumping from Brazil's lap to retrieve it.

"Um let's not!" Brazil said and meant it.

"Scared are we?" Koral butted in.

"Not at all. I just have a better game is all. How about a little CDD? Brazil suggested.

"What is that?" Koral and I said at the same time.

Laughing out loud Brazil said. "Can't believe you two do not know about it. CDD is short for confess, drink or dare!"

"How do you play?" Koral asked all excited.

"We get a bottle of alcohol and the person holding the bottle will ask a question that they too will have to answer. If you do not want to answer then you take a drink from the bottle or offer to take on a dare from the person on her right."

"Sounds a lot like Truth or Dare to me." Koral teased.

"Well it's not, it has drinking in it and you have to answer your own questions. I like it. Let's play." I said.

I went to retrieve a bottle of Tequila from the kitchen.

It was pitch black in the house aside from a few dimmed lights coming in from the streets. I had to feel my way to and from the kitchen. I asked Koral and Brazil to follow me to the ceremonial room. Once we entered the room, I lit a few candles for us to be able to see. Playing in the ceremonial room gave the game a spiritual twist.

I invited Koral and Brazil into the circle after blessing it.

"Whatever happens in this circle stays in this circle." I said laughing.

Brazil and Koral agreed and the game got started. The questions started off silly as ever. Koral asked us about our first kiss which we all answered more than willingly. Then things picked up and we all started taking drinks when asked to share our darkest secrets. Finally once we were all drunk the sex questions came and the dares were being taken for the hell of it.

It was damn near two in the morning and we were still playing. I could not believe how drastic things had changed from Koral and I fighting to the three of us now laughing like old friends. For that night we were able to forget about all the mess that surrounded us in the real word. The lightning had stopped but the rain was steady against the windowpane.

"Koral, I dare you to kiss Brazil passionately in the mouth." I said.

Both Koral and Brazil looked to me with wide eyes and opened mouths. I smiled a sexy smile and gave them both the okay to proceed. Koral knew that I was down with a threesome. I had asked her to join me in one before, just not with a woman. Brazil and I had discussed her having one and how I would be down to do the same with the right group of women. The right women were right next to me. I had my best friend that I had loved for life and my new lover. They were two very sexy women that could have their way with me. This was going to be good and I planned to enjoy every drop of it.

Koral kneeled before Brazil as she had kneeled before me many of times. A simple kiss led to more kissing, and more kissing led to stripping away clothing and touching dares. There we were, the three of us, Koral, Brazil and I all naked and touching, sucking and kissing whatever was in our view. The candle light danced between us as we made some heat of our own.

I watched Brazil massage Koral's pussy with her hand. Koral was so wet. I could hear it more than I could see it. The candlelight was burning low but I was still able to see what I needed to. Koral's lips were whispering something only nothing came out. I decided to just watch for a while. Things were getting heated up and I wondered if we all would be able to go back to normal after that night. I was the only woman that Koral had ever been with but she seemed to be enjoying Brazil just the same.

When I went to read her mind, it was then that I knew she was pretending that it was just the two of us. She would do anything to please me. She felt being with Brazil and I was payback for fucking up my night. It was a good way to start making up but nothing could replace my desire to murder but murder itself.

I continued to watch Brazil's beautiful naturally tanned skin against Koral's smooth and flawless mocha body that smelled of cocoa butter. Brazil's tongue was now teasing the wet hairs on Koral's vagina. It caused Koral to moan pleasurable sounds throughout the ceremonial room.

Koral's body moved slightly as a response to Brazils touch. Brazil leaned further over Koral's body and placed her head perfectly between Koral's gapped legs. I watched my lovers love on each other.

I waited for the right time to join them. I crawled closer to them and made my way between Koral's legs to greet Brazil's head. She looked up from Koral's pussy to kiss me with the same scent that was coming from between Koral's thighs. My tongue met Brazil's and we did a tongue dance before she drowned me with Koral's sweet and familiar scent.

I removed my lips from Brazil's to taste Koral. Her scent on Brazil's lips left me wanting the real thing. Brazil repositioned to share another sensual kiss with Koral. I loved hearing their lips together. I thought about how the three of us would make great serial killers and no one would ever suspect good old Koral and the model cop Brazil. I could surely hide behind their self-righteous identities and lick on their pussies for the rest of my life.

Brazil called me over to her and I crawled to my lover. I laid my head in her bare lap enjoying the smell of her wetness. I looked up into her eyes that were looking down into mine, as her hands went from massaging Koral's full breast to cupping my small ones. Koral sat up and leaned her nakedness against Brazil to watch her fondle me. Brazil's hands were at my weakest spot. It excited me to no return to have Koral watching. She was more than familiar with what rubbing my stomach did to me. I could sense a bit of rage in her passionate filled brown eyes. As much as Koral hated watching Brazil love on me, she enjoyed it the same and wouldn't turn away or leave.

No one spoke a word but the silent thoughts in the room were vibrating off the walls and I could hear them all so very clearly. The only sounds being made were those of pleasure and wet lips and pussy.

Brazil moved over to the other side of my body opposite Koral and started teasing my nipples with her teeth. I squirmed beneath her while allowing my legs to fall apart. I was ready and waiting for whatever. I rubbed myself as Brazil touched and kissed me all over. I played in her hair until it fell from the cropped ponytail that she kept it in. My body continued to move according to her touch.

Brazil lay on her back and invited me to sit over her head. I barely got my legs over her head before she pulled me down on to her face and into her warm mouth. I called Koral to me with just a gesture of my hand. She gave me her mouth to tongue fuck, while I continued to ride Brazil's face.

Koral played in my crimson locs and teased my ear with her warm and plumped lips. We were a long way from ending the night. Before we separated that night both Koral and I would drain Brazil's body together. We showed our gratitude for Brazil being so damn generous with her sexual appetite. For a moment I wanted it all to be a wet dream that I would wake up from. But I did not believe in regrets and so after the moment passed, I was willing to deal with whatever I had to. It had been such an amazing and erotic filled night with two gorgeous women that I loved and was beginning to love dearly.

∞

The next afternoon came without notice. I woke to heavy sobbing coming from somewhere closer than Koral's room. I looked over at Brazil who was still asleep and got out of bed to go and check on Koral. I was hoping that she just had a hangover. Though, I kind of figured that she would end up having an issue with what went down between the three of us the night before. I wondered why it had to be anything but a beautiful thing that we had experienced together. Then it hit me that she probably wanted to be the one I woke up with.

I knocked on the bathroom door before walking in. Koral was in the shower crying. I sat on the commode to urinate and to find out what exactly was going on with her now.

"Let's talk." I said while rubbing my eyes with one hand and flushing the toilet with the other.

Koral peeped from behind the shower curtains with red eyes and a wet face. "Okay."

"What is wrong Koral? Is it last night?"

"Yes and no. I do not like being the one left alone."

I sighed deeply. "I am sorry. It won't happen again."

Koral continued. "And I just cannot shake the feeling that something bad happened to Paul right here in this very house that I am sleeping in."

I could not believe that she was starting the Pierre thing again and so very early in the morning.

"Koral, lower your voice, Brazil is still here and the walls are thin." I whispered.

Then she just up and asked me what she had to have been thinking all along.

"Scarlet, did you kill Paul?"

I covered my mouth and then looked to Koral in shock and stood up from the toilet.

"Do you think I could have killed Pierre without any help?"
She shrugged her shoulders. "That is not an answer Scarlet."
"I would have needed you Koral. I have been waiting on you all this time because murder is not something I can do alone."

Koral, of all people, standing in my shower, accusing me of murder, I never thought I would see the day when I had to defend myself to my best friend. It actually made me sad.

"I can't figure it all out. But what I do know is that Paul's keychain was intact the day before. I just do not know how it got under your bed." Koral said a little too loud before sobbing again.
"Okay! Just stop talking about this. I know how it looks. We need to talk about this alone. Don't you have to work?"
"Yes, a little later. I could not sleep."

I had to shut her up and so I told Koral what she wanted to hear. I said that I loved her and I would never do anything consciously that would hurt her. I promised her that we would talk alone when she returned from work and that Brazil would not be there.
"I want to fix things between us and I know that I can tell you anything."

Koral blinked her eyes at me but did not respond. I leaned in to kiss her on the forehead before turning to wash my hands and leaving the bathroom.
As soon as I went to open my bedroom door Brazil damn near yanked me in and was all over me with questions.

"What the fuck Scarlet? Is Koral accusing you of murdering that dude? I could not make it all out but what the fuck?"

I had a feeling that Brazil was up and listening, Koral had such a big ass mouth.

"Are you spying on me now?"

"Fuck no, but I am glad that I was able to hear what I did. Now explain what the fuck is going on."

Now Brazil was suspicious. I had to get control of this situation. It was just too damn early to think clearly but I had to get my shit together quickly.

"Explain?"

Brazil's eyebrow raised up and her nose flared out.

"My ass and my career could be on the line. Do you have any idea what they do to ex cops in jail?"

"Who said anything about jail? Chill the fuck out? I have this under control."

"How so?"

"I'm going to tell Koral the truth and she will understand and then we can put this behind us and she will stop looking for Pierre then as well. "

Brazil was not too keen on me talking to Koral about Pierre's murder. I had to end up giving her my word that I would never involve her or let Koral know that she knew anything about it. Brazil was convinced since she overheard me tell Koral that I did not want her to hear our conversation. *I need to figure this shit out quick before these broads figure out that I'm lying about something.*

Chapter Eighteen
Koral

Scarlet showed up at my job right before it was time for me to get off. We had the doors locked and were cleaning up the restaurant when I spotted Scarlet's cherry locs and pale face pressed up against the double glass doors. She was waving and smiling. I knew that something had to be out of the ordinary because Scarlet had never come to get me from work. I opened the door to let her know that I would be out soon and noticed a yellow cab parked and waiting.

"Hey Scarlet." I said giving her a hug. What are you doing here?" I said looking behind her at the familiar cab driver.

"My friend Philly came to the house to visit and I asked if we could scoop you from work to save you a fare. You remember Philly don't you Koral?" She said all suspicious.

I glanced in his direction and he waved. The tattoos and bearded chin helped me to remember him. He had dropped me home one night from the club. I did not know that he and Scarlet were friends but it did not surprise me either.

I waved in his direction and looked at Scarlet. "Okay, give me fifteen minutes and I will be ready. "

"Sure thing." She said and twisted her little body back toward the cab.

Exactly fifteen minutes later Gray and I said our goodbyes. He said that it was a little chilly and that he would be waiting for his wife inside. I walked to the cab with the driver looking at me with lust filled eyes. I hoped and prayed that Scarlet had not planned another threesome that I really was not in the mood for. I had too many questions that she had the answer to. All I wanted that night was to talk to my best friend about what had happened to Paul. I noticed a brown paper bag on the back of the seat when I entered the cab and wondered what the hell I had just gotten into.

"We are going to make a stop before we go home okay?" Scarlet told me while pretending to ask.
"Okay." I said apprehensively.

I was quiet for most of the ride and Scarlet kept looking back at me and smiling. We reached the Riverwalk and parked. Scarlet and Philly got out of the car and asked me to join them. We walked along the Riverwalk with only the lamppost to guide us. It was quiet and not a soul was in sight. It was close to midnight at least. I was tired and my feet were still hurting a bit from standing all night at work. Whatever we were here for I prayed that it would be over soon. Then I started thinking that maybe Philly had helped Scarlet get rid of Paul and they were about to tell me what happened.

Philly pulled out a joint and lit it while inhaling.

"You look like you need it." Philly said passing the joint to me.
I did need it for so many reasons. "Thank you." I said.

I took the joint from Philly and pulled on it a few times before passing it back.

I needed the peace it would bring to my raging mind. Philly lit another and gave it to Scarlet and a rotation of two joints started.

Scarlet came over and hugged me. I felt her slip something in my jacket's pocket. She whispered in my ear.

"Place it in the drink." She said to me.

I did not understand at the moment but knew that I was in the midst of Scarlet's mess.

"What are you two whispering about?" Philly said from the sideline.

"Just trying to get my girl to get on chill mode so that we can have a good time." Scarlet said to him smiling.

"Oh good. This is definitely my fantasy come true. Two hot chicks in the back of my cab on a starry night on the Riverwalk." Philly said laughing.

I was not amused at all and hoped like hell that he was not expecting me to fuck him after just getting off work and never mind that it was not my idea. There was no telling what Scarlet had told him without bothering to get my permission.

"Koral, there is some cognac in a brown paper bag on the backseat of the cab. Why don't you go make us all a drink while I speak to Philly for a moment in private," Scarlet said.

"Sure." I said.

I did not want to do what Scarlet had asked but also did not want to end up making her mad. If Scarlet got mad, I could forget about her telling me anything about Paul. I owed Paul at least that. I would find out what happened to him at all cost.

I walked back to the car and sat inside to make the drinks. I guess I took a lil longer than Scarlet wanted because she was at the car window watching me when I looked up.

"I told him that you may need help with carrying three cups." Scarlet said smiling.

I smiled because I was finally feeling the effects of the weed. I took a long sip of the gin from the bottle before handing Scarlet two cups.

"Dang Koral, take it easy. I do not need you drunk right now." She teased but was also serious.

"Don't worry. I'm just feeling good all of a sudden."

"Good. Now put what I gave you in that drink. I already crushed them up."

I pulled a powdery substance from a small plastic bag and looked to Scarlet.

"We are just going to have some fun. Philly isn't fucking anything tonight and will hope like hell that he had listened when I asked him not to show up at my place unannounced.

Scarlet laughed her wicked laugh.

"Good."

"He has disrespected me twice after being asked to respect my right to privacy."

I breathed a little easier knowing that we were only going to have fun, although, I was not in the mood for that either. I guess we were going to pull one of our old tricks of abandoning a hopeful guy that was out of control. I relaxed a bit and added some of the powder to Philly's drink.

"Put it all in." Scarlet demanded when I went to put the powder back into my pocket.

I hesitated and then did as she said while thinking that it was enough in that bag to kill a horse if it was anything harmful at all. I dare ask Scarlet any questions. I said a silent prayer and got out of the car with the drink.

"Give me the bag. I'll get rid of it." Scarlet advised.

I said okay and handed her the small plastic bag. We walked back toward Philly and he eagerly went to Scarlet for his drink.

"Koral has yours. You said to make it extra strong. These in my hand are girly drinks. "Don't take us much." Scarlet said winking.

Philly laughed and took the cup from my hand.

"Thank you Koral." He said and gulped the drink down to prove his manhood.

Moments later Philly started grabbing his dick and telling Scarlet and I all the perverted things he wanted to do to us. He started pulling on us and attempting to kiss the both of us. I kept fighting him off and Scarlet gave in a few times to settle him down. She walked him up by a lamppost right in front of the river. They kissed and rubbed bodies there for a while before Philly requested that we return to the cab.

"Let's go get in the back of the cab." He barely managed while swaying.

I stood there unable to move and wondering what the fuck was going to happen next.

"Not just yet. Besides, I rather you bend me over the back of the cab and fuck me in the opening," Scarlet teased.

"What about Koral?" He said stumbling backwards with Scarlet guiding him closer to the edge of the grass off of the sidewalk and near the water. I knew then that this was not going to end up good.

"Koral come here." Scarlet called as I stood frozen.

Scarlet yelled my name again as she struggled to hold Philly up with her tiny frame. I finally went to her thinking that we would help him to the ground and leave him there.

"Help me dammit!" She said.
"What do you want me to do Scarlet?"
"Take his arm." She said.

Philly fought to stay awake and to make more sexual advances towards us. Philly leaned over on me and put his arm around my shoulder. "I can't wait to dig all up inside your snatch." He whispered before closing his eyes again.

We were facing the side walk with Philly between the both of us when I tried walking forward but Scarlet said to hold on to Philly and to turn around.

"Are we going to lay him on the edge of the grass?" I asked nervously.
"Yes Koral."

At that moment Philly's weight took us all to the ground.

"Help me." Scarlet said trying to roll Philly closer to the edge. I did help her move him closer but then I stopped and refused to push him any further. Scarlet looked to me and sucked her teeth before struggling to roll Philly's body on her own.

"If you don't help, we will be leaving a dead body out in the opening. I can't do this alone Koral and you gave me your word." Scarlet pleaded.

I could not believe that this was actually happening. How dare her force this on me like that?

"I know but I wasn't prepared and you lied to me Scarlet."

"You would've never been prepared and I knew this would be the only way that you would honor your own word."

"This was unfair."

Scarlet hunched her shoulders. "Okay, maybe it was but we have done it now."

"He is not dead."

"He will be soon. Now help me."

Out of fear and wanting it to be over with, I helped Scarlet roll Philly's body into the river. I cried softly at my own stupidity. Philly's body made a loud plop before submerging in the cold water. His eyes popped open in shock or fear before they closed again. I looked to Scarlet and her face was that of pleasure and curiosity. It sickened me to see that. My stomach was in knots and I felt sick but knew better than to vomit.

We walked back to the sidewalk, gathered the cups and went back to the cab to get our things. Scarlet cleaned the cab of finger prints. I watched her walk back to the river with the liquor bottle. She poured the liquor into the river and sat the bottle on the edge of the banks after wiping it off.

I stood in a trance not believing what had just happened. The last two nights were just as unbelievable to me as Paul's disappearance had been and still I had no answers but had just helped Scarlet commit murder for no reason at all. I was knee deep in her mess and did not know how I would get out of it. Scarlet shook me out of my trance.

"We have to leave now." She said pulling me along with her.

It took us over an hour to reach home but we got there. Scarlet said that we could not chance a cab and the buses had stopped running by then. My feet were throbbing by the time we reached the house that night. All I wanted was to be alone but Scarlet insisted that we showered and slept together that night.

"Thank you." She whispered from behind me.

"For what?"

"For proving your unconditional love to me. I would do anything for you Koral and I know now that you would for me also."

I thought about Scarlet's words and how I had lived my entire existence on needing to be loved by her. I thought about how she had loved me and how before tonight I would have done anything for her and could not believe that she had doubt. It was definitely my fault for leading her to believe that I was okay with murdering someone.

I did make Scarlet that promise and I even convinced myself that I was willing to snatch the breath from an innocent person in the name of love. Scarlet was not the enemy, she was just a lost soul like Nana had warned me and I had decided to feed her flame. It was time that I either started to enjoy burning in her fire or put it out altogether. I turned to kiss her because my heart still pulled in her direction.

"I love you more than anything Scarlet Rose Laveau, never doubt that again."

"I don't doubt it now Koral Baptiste." She said.

Her big and bright eyes shone through the dark and stirred the butterflies in my womb.

∞

The sun crept in like a thief early the next morning. I woke to see Scarlet's naked back sitting on the edge of the bed. It was her that was crying this time. Scarlet rarely cried for any reason and so I was deeply concerned.

"Scarlet, what is it?" I asked sitting up and rubbing the sleep from my eyes.

Her back stayed turned away from me. "I killed Pierre."

I was shocked at her confession but not at her deed. "What do you mean, why would you, and how?" I said going to her and kneeling before her body as if it were an altar.

I wanted to scream out but I needed to not only find out the truth about Paul but be there for a friend who had always been there for me. If I was going to help her get help, I would need her to confess her crime.

"It has been so difficult keeping this from you. He was going to hurt me Koral." She said and started sobbing heavily.
"Paul? Hurt you how?"

Scarlet told me that she had heard something in my bedroom that night and thought it was Nana roaming again from missing me. But when she opened the room door Paul was in there and she got angry and started cursing at him and he retaliated. She said he called her awful names and she told him how she fucked me better than he ever did. She said to Paul that my love for her was more than he could ever have with me. Scarlet's words must have hit him deep because he blamed her for us not being married and still in New Orleans. Paul rushed after her and she ran into the living room where she had been before having a drink. I could not believe what I was hearing but knew it to be true from my knowledge of both Paul and Scarlet.

"Then Paul grabbed me by the hair and started to choke me. That is when I managed to get a hold of the liquor bottle and hit him in the head with it.

I held my heart in place. "Dear Jesus."

"He fell and hit his head on the end of the table. I went to him to help Koral but he was dead."

"Oh my God." I said as the tears ran the length of my face.

I did not know who to feel sorry for. The man I had led on or the woman that I loved being attacked by him.

"But who helped you with his body?"

"Philly did and it was the reason he had been blackmailing me to fuck the two of us together."

"I figured that last night."

"He showed up to the house right after it happened and I didn't know what else to do and I didn't want to involve you Koral. You had just lost Nana. I was protecting you."

"I'm so sorry Scarlet, I wish you would have come to me."

"I wish I would have to. I'm sorry Koral," She cried.

I told her that it was not her fault and that we would figure it all out together. I comforted my lover and friend and felt bad for the mess I had made of her and Paul. It was my fault that Paul was dead and I would have to live with that for the rest of my life.

"We will talk more later, I need a moment to myself Scarlet." I said rubbing her arm.

"Yes, I understand." Scarlet said standing to leave.

We hugged and she left.

I laid back in bed sobbing and mourned the memory of Paul. I could not get the thought of him choking Scarlet out of my head. I just could not imagine him getting so angry, he had to have been fed up with it all and who would not be at some point? I hated what he did but I could not hate Paul. He had made a mistake and paid dearly for it.

I must have drifted off and went back to sleep for hours. By the time I woke up I was running late for work again. I showered and called a cab. There was no time for a bus trip. I dressed quickly and ran out the front door to wait for my ride.

I arrived at work only to greet Gray standing out near the door smoking a cigarette and looking like he had lost his best friend.

"Hi Gray." I said leaning in for a hug.

"Hey red eyes. You must have heard?"

"Heard what?"

"You have been crying because you got fired, right?"

"No!" I said.

"My big mouth. Well that is what you are about to walk into. He has already replaced you with some gal looking for a job this morning."

I removed my purse from my shoulder and wiped away at my wet eyes.

"Well damn, this day just keeps getting worse. I guess I can't blame him."

"I guess not. What is going on with you anyhow? It's not like you to keep being late." Gray said putting his cigarette out.

"It's Scarlet again. Something terrible has happened and it is all my fault."

"Look here, I do not need all the details but I do know ain't nothing all your fault. And I know I promised not to speak ill of you friend but I got to Koral."

I shook my head and listened to what Gray had to say.

"Okay Gray."

"You take your responsibility in it all and you cut ties with that evil woman for good before you lose more than your job. Now I gotta get back in here. Take care of yourself and don't you be a stranger."

I hugged Gray tightly and went in to get my last check before walking to the bus stop. I thought about everything all over again and decided what to do about it. I would do what Gray had suggested and take responsibility for my part.

I got off the bus and walked down the same street that I had walked for years. I could see Scarlet with one of her clients on the front porch. They must have been finishing up a session because the gentleman was leaving as I approached.

Scarlet had a look of confusion on her face as I walked up the stairs and before she had time to ask I confessed.

"I lost my job."

"Ahhh Koral. She said hugging me. "There are others.""

"Yes I know but I won't need one."

"What do you mean?"

"I'm going to turn myself in for the murder of Philly and also as punishment for what happened between you and Paul. That was totally my fault."

Scarlet grabbed my arm and pulled me toward the door of the house.

"Have you lost your fucking mind? Come into the house!"

I followed Scarlet in. "I won't implicate you in any way but I must confess my sins. I won't be able to live with what all has happened Scarlet."

Scarlet turned completely red. "You will shut your fucking mouth and never speak of any of this again. Do you understand me?"

I stood there staring at the rage that had gathered on Scarlet's face and started to tremble a bit. I was afraid to do anything but obey.

"Yes."

"I'm not fucking around Koral. You do what I say or else. This is my life that you are fucking with. Don't be stupid now."

I stood there listening to Scarlet and I remembered the satisfaction on her face when we killed Philly and wondered if she wore the same expression when Paul died. I walked away from her as she continued to talk.

"Maybe it is best that you take some time off from working. You have money saved. And I will always help you."

"Maybe I should, I'm going to lay down for a spell." I said defeated.

Chapter Nineteen
Scarlet

Koral was losing it and my life was dangling in the palms of her guilt ridden hands. I was sort of grateful that she had lost her job. The last thing I needed at the moment was for Koral to run her mouth to one of those folks down at that restaurant. I wanted her to stay close to home so that I could keep a better eye on her. I figured that time healed all things and time is what she needed to come to her senses. I knew for sure that she was not the murdering kind and of that I would never ask for her assistance again. You can never panic when control is needed. We lose out on most things in life because we become afraid of the very control that we are capable of having. Koral was like having a child to care for. Not only did I have to protect myself but Koral as well. She was definitely not capable of doing so.

I walked to a local mom and pop store to buy groceries. I stopped along the way and was speaking to Lilia. She was out walking Dexter as usual.

"Can't you help me go home Scarlet. I'm tired and Dexter is missing my folks an awful lot." Lilia said.

My heart ached for Lilia and Dexter.

"Lilia, your parents miss the both of you so much and one day you all will be together again. But for now you need to rest and allow them to rest so that you all will have the strength when the time comes."

"Will it be a long time?"

"A little long. But if you rest you won't notice it at all."

"I will try. After I try going home a few more times for Dexter. He refuses to give up." She said smiling.

I smiled at the lovely ghost of a girl and watched her try and cross the street to her home once more.

I headed in the direction of my home and noticed Brazil's car. I did not understand her being there. I told her that I would be out for a while and that Koral was at home resting. My curiosity took over as I approached my home. I walked down my entry way right into the house without any notice. The house was empty and oddly quiet to have two people in it. Koral had to have let Brazil in. I wondered if they were fucking and headed to her room. *If they wanted to be together again all they had to do was ask.*

I went straight to Koral's room, there was not a soul in there and so I went to my room. *How dare they fuck in my bed!* I pushed my room door open to find it empty but I heard voices outside my window. I stood at the window watching Koral dig around in my garden. She was crying her eyes out. Brazil kneeled down beside her with a look of concern and fright.

I decided to be still and listen. I did not want to interrupt what had already been started. *Watch your prey and only attack with certainty.* The window was wide open and I could hear everything.

"Are you certain that she killed Paul?" Brazil asked.

Koral shook her head yes. "With the guy Philly's help."

"The other guy the two of you killed?"

"That's right. Brazil, I did not know who else to call and I did not want to go to some random police officer with this."

Brazil comforted her by patting Koral on the back. "You did the right thing."

"And I know that you tried to help me find Paul and so I called you for help. I'm sorry for involving you but I'm so scared and lost. I love Scarlet and I know that this is not all her fault."

"It is okay. I can help the two of you if you let me. Do not let Scarlet know that you have spoken to me until I can figure this out. Talk to no one. But you have to pull yourself together some or Scarlet will suspect something is wrong."

"I understand. And thank you." Koral said still crying and clawing my garden to death.

I could not believe that this stupid bitch was telling everything to Brazil after I told her to keep her fucking mouth closed. And just what would Brazil do after finding out I had murdered another person. Things were spiraling out of control right before my eyes. I could lose my new lover, my best friend and my life if I didn't play my cards exactly right. I needed time to think but I did not have any time to waste. I watched Brazil comfort Koral a bit more before I eased back out the door with groceries in hand.

I walked back out the house and down the block a bit before I started to sing loud enough to be heard. By the time I reached my door for a second time Brazil was standing behind the screened door smiling as best as she could and welcomed me in the house.

"I came by wanting to surprise you and found your dear friend in the backyard over Paul's grave. Want to explain?" She asked.

Brazil did not bother to help me with my bags. I walked past her to put the groceries in the kitchen. Brazil was in tow.

"Scarlet, this is not a fucking game."

"I know Brazil, I know." I said before turning to her.

"Koral has no idea that Paul's body is in that ground. It is her way of feeling close to her Nana is all."

I motioned for Brazil to follow me to my room and she did. I closed the door behind her. I had plans to tell her everything. Well at least my version of everything. Brazil had just as much to lose as I did and unlike Koral she did not want to be near a jail. I would just have to use what I knew to get what I wanted.

"I killed someone the other night." I said to Brazil not looking in her direction.

"What do you mean?" She replied trying to seem shocked.

"The guy that interrupted our supper. He had been nosing around here lately and claimed to have seen you and I burying a body in the backyard the night of Pierre's death.

Brazil started pacing the floor. "What the fuck?"

"He said he could tell by the shape of what we put in the barrel that it was a body and was going to the police." I lied.

"What? Why didn't you tell me? Did he want money or just to tell?"

"He wanted me. And I would have did what he wanted but I could not be sure that he would not turn around and tell anyhow."

Brazil bit down on her bottom lip and continued to pace.

"Right. Continue please."

"And I had involved you enough. I couldn't let you go to jail for my mistake. And you see I couldn't tell Koral the truth but I needed her help."

"Oh baby. I'm so sorry you had to do all that alone. I was thinking all sorts of crazy shit."

Brazil and I discussed everything and decided the best thing to do was to make it all go away. I allowed Koral to continue confessing to Brazil while I thought of a way out of the madness that I had allowed to escape my control. Decisions had to be made and I had to make them before Koral and Brazil compared notes and figured out my lies.

Chapter Twenty
Roses Have Thorns

Like any other rose I bloomed into a world accepting of my beauty but ignorant to my influence. Roses have thorns to remind us that everything comes with a price, even love. I gave love unconditionally and only expected it back in return. Koral had betrayed me even after proving that she did love me. I knew her love was true and that she would be willing to take the fall and do time in the name of that very love for me. But I also knew that no one in their right mind would believe that Koral could pull off a murder alone. And for that reason alone I had to make sure that Koral would stop talking and find peace with what had happened. We still had our entire life to live and I for one wanted to live mine to the fullest.

I dressed in my ritual clothing in front of a full length mirror. I wanted to take a good long look at my whole self because the next sun would shine on a new me. A Scarlet that understood that with all the pleasure in the world comes the pain.

My plans were to visit a spirit house and a drumming circle later that evening. But first, I had business to take care of with Carmelite. She was on her way to the house for a reading before I left that evening. As I walked down the hall the phone started ringing and I almost ignored it but something pulled me to it.

"Laveau's residence."

"Hey baby Laveau." My daddy sounded somewhat cheerful.

I did not have the time or the patience for more than my daddy's love at that moment.

"Hi Daddy Laveau." I responded as he would wish.

"What you up to?" He pried.

"About to do a reading for Carmelite."

"I see. Send her our love. I won't hold you. Your momma and I were baking cookies and started down memory lane. I love you baby girl, that is all. Going to put your momma on now."

"I love you too daddy man." I teased.

Momma Laveau got on the phone talking cookie dough and I could hear my daddy telling her that I did not have time for all that. I chuckled a little.

"Hey sweet girl." Momma Laveau said.

They killed me with all that baby shit at times. I was a full grown woman but did not have it in me to be mean to my folks.

"Hi Momma Laveau, you good?"

"Concerned about you. Is everything okay, I mean really? I been dreaming about you coming to visit us and when we open the door to greet you… you reach for us and your hands are all covered in blood."

"Momma you know as well as I do that we cause ourselves to dream. So I should be asking what is up with you?"

Momma Laveau got quiet and breathed in deeply. "Don't try pulling that with me. I gave you the gift that you have child."

"Yes momma I know. Look everything is fine. Carmelite is here and waiting." I lied. "How about I come for a visit real soon?"

Momma Laveau broke out in laughter. I could hear her clapping. She repeated what I had said to Daddy Laveau and then she got back on the phone.

"There is so much I want to do with you here and we miss you an awful lot. Maybe you will even consider moving here."

"Do not push me momma. Now I love you, give daddy my love, talk to you soon."

Daddy Laveau was asking Momma Laveau a thousand questions as I hung up the phone. I walked to the front of the house and sat down at the table and waited for Carmelite. A few minutes later the half charred face of Carmelite appeared at the screen door and I called for her to come in.

"My parents send their love Carmelite." I said as she took a seat across from me.

"Awww. Send mine back and let em know they sure is missed round here."

"I will. Shall we get started?" I asked.

Carmelite shook her head yes and we began our journey.

I fell into a trance quickly. Lisette seemed to be waiting for me that day. Something had changed about her and I felt a second death surrounding her heavy frame. The eyes in her beautiful face were now dark as coal.

"My momma can feel safe now. Henri is dead." She said.

"Dead?"

"Yes. I scared him til his heart fell silent."

"I see. How do you feel?"

"Like I died a second time? But my misery is worth my momma's safety." She said.

"Indeed it is child. Come with me."

"No. I am done with the visits. You tell my momma goodbye for me. Tell her I cannot come back no more."

With that Lisette walked away in the grayest space I have ever seen. My dark heart wore a ton for her and Carmelite. I turn around to face myself and woke up. Carmelite sat eager.

"I'm sorry Carmelite. Lisette is not coming."

"Bad day for you?" Carmelite asked looking confused.

"No. I found her. She is doing real good but has gone too far away for me to bring back."

I looked away from Carmelite's eyes not wanting to lie to her face. She shook her head at me.

"Is that so?"

"Lisette has entered a permanent resting place and wants you to do the same. She said not to be afraid that she would see you again soon."

"That is all… that is it?"

I kept trying to talk over Carmelite.

"She said you can feel safe now."

"What that mean?'

I looked out the window not wanting to answer.

"I knows what Lisette did and it ain't right, you don't do evil for evil. She never rest like that and now she shame to come back, ain't that the truth Scarlet? Ain't it?"

I looked back at Carmelite and saw the softer side of a heart that I was not given and neither had Lisette or Henri known of a heart of such.

"Yes Carmelite. That is right."

"The social worker tell me Henri dead and all he had is mine now and he had money saved. I tell her nothing he had I want but my Lisette. I knew then Lisette done it."

I wanted to comfort her. Tell her something to settle her heavy heart. I just wanted to take her pain away. Carmelite just did not deserve any of it.

"Better days are ahead Carmelite. You just keep on living and you shall see."

"It was my job to be Lisette's protector, not her mine. I tried telling my girl that didn't I Scarlet?" Carmelite said with tears falling.

Tears fell from my own eyes. "Yes you did."

"Henri died clutching a bible. They say he was white as a ghost with his eyes and mouth stretched opened. I knew his heart was stopped by his own daughter."

"Carmelite." I said rubbing her hand and trying to console her but she would not stop talking.

She got up from the table. "Good evening Ms. Scarlet. This be our last session and I thank you." She said and headed out the door.

I stood up and went to look after her. I knew that she had plans on joining Lisette and there was nothing I could do to stop her. Paths are lain for some to walk them straight through without any bends or turns, such was Carmelite's.

As Carmelite disappeared in the dark and distance I locked the front door behind me with Koral on the other side hiding out in her room from me. She had been avoiding me as much as possible since confessing my crimes to Brazil. Koral probably assumed that I would be able to read what she had done. I laughed a little before trying to squeeze tears from my eyes. It was a damn shame because I loved Koral most of all.

It was getting really cold out. I pulled my coat on and buttoned it up around my neck. I noticed Nana sitting on the porch as I walked down the steps. I turned around to face her.

"I told you that you do not scare me." I said before leaving.

I arrived at the spiritual house and knocked three times before entering. It was a sign of respect, gave the Spirits a chance to undress. Just as knocking on my door gave me time to dress. You never wanted to enter anybody's house without knocking, because you may see some shit you do not want to. I stayed there for a couple of hours as planned.

After leaving the spirit house I headed down the street and around the corner to meet Brazil. I told her to meet me at the park over there. I sat on the swing going over everything a thousand times trying to align them with the stars.

Brazil pulled up twenty minutes later and took a seat on the swing next to me.

"You're late."

"Yes, I know and I apologize. Koral called no sooner than you left as you expected. She asked me to come over and I did."

"And?" I said with all the patience of Job.

"And, when I got there she asked me to take her under arrest for the murder of the Philly guy."

"Worse than I thought." I said shaking my head.

"I told her that we should talk because she needed to know things about him, like his real name in order to file a report."

My heart was breaking to hear this. What would become of us?

"I cannot believe this is happening."

Several tears finally fell from my eyes. It was more than I had probably cried in my life time. I guess my soul was stirring.

Brazil continued. "She insisted that I take her to the police station or that she would go on her own. Koral said that Paul and Philly's spirits were in the house and she could not be there another night."

"Where is she now?"

Brazil reached out to soothe the side of my face with her cold hand.

"At my place waiting for me to come back with a report for her to fill out and then place her under arrest."

"My god! Take me to my friend." I said and headed toward Brazil's car.

Koral was lying on the sofa when we arrived at Brazil's house. Her skin was almost transparent against the dark brown sofa. She did not look surprised at all to see me. She sat up to make room for me. I took a seat next to my beautiful friend and wrapped an arm around her. I laid my head against her chest and listened to her heartbeat.

"Remember when we were kids and I would lay on you and listen to your heart tell me stories that I would then repeat to you?"

"Yes, I wish we could go back to that time." Koral said as she played in my locs.

"Sadly time is the only thing we cannot control my love."

"Scarlet, I'm sorry but I have to do this. I pray that you will forgive me one day?"

I sat up to grab her lips with mine and she kissed me back in a sad goodbye kind of way. I knew then that there was nothing I could say to change her mind.

"I hope that you can forgive me too. I love you to death Koral." I said as my eyes danced with her shiny wet ones.
"I love you too." Koral replied.

I smiled and soothed the side of her face with my hand as I always did. Her skin was perfect in color and warm to the touch. Brazil stood silently behind Koral. I looked up to give her the okay and she slid the plastic bag over Koral's head. Before I could remove my hand from her face I felt her hot tears on the back of my hand. I slid it from beneath the bag and fingered the wetness on the back of my hand. I watched as Koral fought to remove the bag that Brazil held tightly around her neck. I laid my head against her chest as she lost the battle and listened to her heart until it stopped.

Brazil wanted to dump Koral's body down in the Mississippi river or better yet the bayou. She said many people were buried there and never heard from again. Maybe because the crocodiles had gotten to them or because the mud was just too thick to ever get to them. I refused to do that to Koral.

I made Brazil help me bring Koral back to our home. She deserved a proper burial. I washed her up and dressed her in something really fancy. I put pearls around her neck and combed her curls that she had allowed to grow out for the first time since we were children. I painted her nails and put perfume on her. Koral looked like Barbie lying there all still and at peace. I cried something awful because I would never be able to love on Koral again and I was going to miss her terribly. *Why did you make me do it Koral? Just why?*

Nana sat rolling her bug eyes at me and shaking her old wrinkled head. Brazil was rushing me to finish up. She had been in the backyard digging another hole to place Koral in. We carried her out and placed her near Pierre. He could finally have her and she could finally be with her family and I would always have her right here with me.

"What will you say if somebody asks after her?" Brazil asked.

"Who would ask? Koral only had me left."

"Your parents."

"I can handle my parents."

"If you say so but make sure you tell me whatever you tell them."

"Okay. I want to put scarlet roses over Koral's grave. She loved roses and she loved me."

"Anything you want Scarlet. Anything you want." Brazil promised.

I looked up at Brazil looking down at me. Her eyes told me that her mouth spoke the truth. What she had for me was unconditional. I reached for her and she helped me up.

"Ready for your first drumming circle?" I asked.

"I am."

Brazil smiled and we headed into the house to wash up and to hurry to the drumming ceremony. I did not know how long we would be together or who I would love tomorrow. But for now, she was the person that I wanted in my life. Brazil was trustworthy and willing to lay down her own body for me. A body that was willing to stand next to mine and join me in every aspect of my world. And most of all, she didn't mind the thorns on my rose.

"The truth is, everyone is going to hurt you. You just got to find the ones worth suffering for."
-**Bob Marley**

www.ingramcontent.com/pod-product-compliance
Lightning Source LLC
Chambersburg PA
CBHW020415180626
46812CB00003B/982